The Vet's Daughter

Other Virago Modern Classics
published by The Dial Press

FROST IN MAY
Antonia White

THE LOST TRAVELLER
Antonia White

BEYOND THE GLASS
Antonia White

THE SUGAR HOUSE
Antonia White

THE JUDGE
Rebecca West

THE UNLIT LAMP
Radclyffe Hall

THE LACQUER LADY
F. Tennyson Jesse

THE BETH BOOK
Sarah Grand

THE GETTING OF WISDOM
Henry Handel Richardson

BARBARA COMYNS

The
Vet's Daughter

With a new introduction by the author

The Dial Press
New York

Published by
The Dial Press
1 Dag Hammarskjold Plaza
New York, New York 10017

Copyright © Barbara Comyns 1959
Introduction Copyright © Barbara Comyns 1981

Library of Congress Cataloging in Publication Data

Comyns, Barbara, 1912–
The vet's daughter.
A Virago modern classic.

I. Title. II. Series.
PR6053.0452V4 1981   823'.914   81-9702
ISBN 0-385-27190-5   AACR-2

Introduction

I WAS BORN IN WARWICKSHIRE in a house on the banks of the Avon and was one of six children. Our father was a semi-retired managing director of a Midland chemical firm. He was an impatient, violent man, alternatively spoiling and frightening us. Our mother was many years younger and lived the life of an invalid most of the time. I remember her best lying in a shaded hammock on one of the lawns, reading and eating cherries, which she was inordinately fond of, or in the winter sitting by the morning-room fire and opening and shutting her hands before the blaze as if to store the heat. Her pet monkey sitting on the fender would be doing the same. When she was about twenty-five she suddenly went completely deaf and we children had to speak to her in deaf and dumb language on our hands. We really had little contact with our mother even before she went deaf and were brought up by our formidable grandmother, governesses and the servants. We seldom mixed with other children and spent most of our time in boats, often fishing. It is extraordinary that none of us were drowned because only two could swim. We were educated by governesses who had few qualifications to teach; some stayed for years and others left pretty quickly. They had names like Miss Glide and Miss Vann, and there was the exotic Miss Bonfellow, who wore a golden plumed hat which she threw in the river when she left.

I started writing at the age of ten, usually illustrating my stories, and I don't know which I enjoyed most, the writing or drawing. At about this time my eldest sister was sent to a famous girl's school, but bewildered and homesick, she ran away after a few days and caused a great panic until she was found on a country railway station eating buns provided by a kindly station master. Eventually some of us, including me, were sent to a boarding school for the Daughters of Gentlemen that was supposed to be a 'home from home'. For some reason we were suddenly taken away when I was aged fifteen. Perhaps there were money difficulties. My father had been living on his capital for years. I had no more education until after his death, when I was old enough to go to an art school. I first went to one in Stratford-on-Avon, then moved to London and went to Heatherley's, in the days when it was just off Baker Street and run by old Mr Massey. At that time it was the only London art school where students could draw from life without first spending a year drawing from the antique, which usually meant plaster casts. I didn't stay at Heatherley's as long as I had hoped because my money ran out.

I managed to get a job in a small advertising agency, drawing, typing, writing simple copy and visiting clients. I was paid a pathetic salary and lived in a small room near Mornington Crescent station costing eleven shillings a week. It was a decaying, gritty district but central, and it pleased me to know that Dickens had once lived there, also several of the characters in his books. I discovered public libraries at this time and read until I was almost drunk on books; but my own writing suffered and became imitative and self-conscious. In the end, with great strength of mind, I destroyed all the stories and half-written novels I'd written over the years when I left my dank bed-sitting room to get married.

I married a young artist that I'd known slightly since we were children – actually, we first met on an Anglo-Saxon burial ground where excavations were going on in a field near my home, but we didn't see much of each other until we went to study art in London. We were both in our early twenties when we married and it was a disaster in many ways, and after two children and many troubles we parted more or less amicably.

During my marriage I worked as an artist's model, sometimes posing with my babies. The pay was very poor and, with two children depending on me, I became a business woman out of desperation, converting old houses into flats and running a garage where I sold elderly, unusual cars, Delages and Lagondas in particular. Things were going fairly well until war loomed nearer and nearer. I lost my tenants and soon no one wanted to buy my magnificent old cars and they were towed away to a breaker's yard.

When the war started I moved to the country with

the children and found a sympathetic family who gave me a wing of their house in return for doing some cooking. The children were happy, which pleased me, but I felt lonely and frustrated until I borrowed a typewriter and started writing again. At first I wrote part of a novel with a wartime background; then I changed my mind and wrote *Sisters by a River* and re-lived my childhood. When it was finished I put it away in a suitcase where I kept old photographs.

We returned to London in 1942. So did many other people and I was able to let my flats again. I bought and sold antique furniture and, even more profitable, grand pianos. I also bred poodles and the money I made from selling the puppies paid the children's school fees. All this time I was writing.

When I was working on *Our Spoons came from Woolworths* an old friend found the MS of *Sisters by a River* when he was looking through the family photographs and thought it should be published. After some false starts it was serialised in *Lilliput*. This resulted in it being published by Eyre and Spottiswoode and, as I had by then finished "Spoons" they accepted both books simultaneously. At the same time I met the man who was to be my second husband. Life was perfect except for flying bombs which started a day or two after our meeting. We were married and went to Snowdonia for our honeymoon, staying in a cottage by a waterfall lent to us by Kim Philby. That is where I got the idea of *The Vet's Daughter*, but I only wrote a few notes at the time and spent the next two years writing a book about Leigh Hunt, covering thirteen years of his life. I did a lot of research, which I loved – it seemed to make up for all the study I'd missed as a girl – but I discovered nothing new about Leigh Hunt and the book never found a publisher.

The next book I wrote was *Who was Changed and Who was Dead*, based on newspaper reports of an epidemic of ergot poisoning in a French village supplemented by accounts in a medical journal. I set it in my childhood village and my imagination took hold of me and it almost wrote itself. When it was finished I went through my old note-books and found the faint framework of *The Vet's Daughter*. I had set it in Wales, with the mother as the main character, but as soon as I started to write, the plot and characters changed and again the book seemed to write itself. I did most of the actual writing from five in the morning until seven, when there was little chance of being disturbed; but it ran through my head all day and at night I dreamt about it, which often meant altering whole chapters of the book the following morning. I could see it all happening as if in a film as I wrote and I spent a considerable amount of time driving and wandering around Battersea and Clapham trying to see it through Alice's eyes.

When the book was published by Heinemann in 1959 it was very well received by the critics and every now and again it appears in a new form, as a serial on the BBC, then as a play and more recently Sandy Wilson turned it into a musical.

Barbara Comyns, 1980

Chapter One

A MAN WITH SMALL EYES and a ginger moustache came and spoke to me when I was thinking of something else. Together we walked down a street that was lined with privet hedges. He told me his wife belonged to the Plymouth Brethren, and I said I was sorry because that is what he seemed to need me to say and I saw he was a poor broken-down sort of creature. If he had been a horse, he would have most likely worn knee-caps. We came to a great red railway arch that crossed the road like a heavy rainbow; and near this arch there was a vet's house with a lamp outside. I said, "You must excuse me," and left this poor man among the privet hedges.

I entered the house. It was my home and it smelt of animals, although there was lino on the floor. In the brown hall my mother was standing; and she looked at me with her sad eyes half-covered by their heavy lids, but did not speak. She just stood there. Her bones were small and her shoulders sloped; her teeth were not straight either; so, if she had been a dog, my father would have destroyed her.

I said, "Mother, I smell cabbage. It must be lunchtime."

She looked scared and scuttled towards the kitchen, holding up her little hands like kitten's paws. I went into the dining-room intending to lay the table, but Mother had been before me, and, although the silver was quite bright, there were brown gravy marks on the table-cloth—even when I arranged salt-cellars over them they were not covered. There were pickles of various colours in jars. The water in the glass jug looked stale; but there was beer for my father.

The dining-room was dark because a dirty holly tree came close to the window. You could not have told it was summer except that the firegrate was filled with pleated paper with soot on it. Before the fireplace was a rug made from a skinned Great Dane dog, and on the carved mantelpiece there was a monkey's skull with a double set of teeth, which seemed to chatter when you looked at them.

The three of us sat round the table eating cold meat. It was Monday. No one spoke a word, and our knives and forks sounded rather loud. Mother dropped a spoon that had mashed potato on it and gave a weak little titter. Father bit his moustache. It was a black one with waxed corners. I knew that in the bathroom cupboard there was a small bottle of colourless liquid with a French label which turned his moustache and eyebrows a startling black; and I wished he wouldn't use it because it somehow seemed wicked.

After lunch I helped Mother in the kitchen. Through the window I could see the sun shining on houses, so I asked Mother if I could walk in the park with my friend Lucy. As usual, she told me to ask Father, so I went to the surgery. The door was propped open by a horse's hoof without a horse joined to it, and I looked through. He was sewing in a Peke's eye. He used chloroform, but I went away because I couldn't bear to see him sewing a dog like that. The smell of chloroform seemed to go with me even when I met my friend.

We walked in Battersea Park. Lucy's hair fell down her back like water from a tap, very straight and long. Mine was like a pale yellow bell. We talked on our hands because Lucy was a deaf mute; her mother was turning her into a dressmaker because she considered it a suitable trade for those that were deaf and dumb. We were both seventeen. Mothers sat on dark green benches watching their children playing on the sooty grass, bowling bright hoops and balls. We went to see the birds, and in the distance a band was playing. Soldiers tried to speak to us until they noticed that we used our hands to speak with. Then we watched the pleasure-steamers and barges on the river. Great bales of different-coloured paper and boats loaded with straw went past very quickly, and a man with a black face in a coal-barge waved to us, and we waved back because we knew he couldn't stop. It was lovely by the water; but too soon it was time to return home through the hot, ugly streets of red and yellow houses. I don't know what happened to Lucy when she went home, but I got a great slap on the back of the head from Father, and was made to clean the cats' cages.

That evening Father went out to play billiards and my mother and I sat peacefully in the back garden, which was made of clinkers entwined with dark ivy. We sewed the holes that come in sheets, and my mother talked about the farm in Wales where she had lived when she was a girl. She told me about huge mountain goats that were wild and had enormous curling horns, and still, dark lakes that were icy-cold from mountain streams, and the waterfall beside the farm which was the only water supply they had. I liked to listen to Mother when she talked; but she only whispered when Father was at home.

The day was nearly over and it was like most of the days I could remember: all overshadowed by my father and cleaning the cats' cages and the smell of cabbage, escaping gas and my father's scent. There were moments of peace, and sometimes sunlight outside. It was like that all the time.

In the morning I would come down the dark brown stairs, and there would be my mother scurrying about, always keeping close to the wall. Her lifeless hair stuck out behind in a battered pigtail that was more like a donkey's tail. She would dart about with brushes and brooms and later with jugs of steaming water for Father's room—and his breakfast, too. Kippers and eggs and crisp, curly bacon would disappear upstairs; but we had damp bread and jam in the kitchen. When the weather was cold we would huddle round the greasy gas stove, and Mother would pull her nasty pink dressing-gown over her poor flat chest.

She would be dressed when Father came down with his firm, heavy tread and the smell of eau-de-Cologne. I would be cleaning the animals' cages. The cats mewed unceasingly, and the dogs—with their sad eyes—barked and howled, always waiting. If it hadn't been a poor neighbourhood, people would have complained. There was a parrot that screamed, too; but its owners paid us eight shillings a week to listen to it, so it was worth it. That morning as I cleaned those cages, I looked at Father as he sat in his office, at his desk. It was a roll-topped desk and somehow looked like an organ. There he sat biting the quicks of his nails, waiting for the man from the vivisectionist who was coming to collect the animals that no one wanted. They were brought to Father to be destroyed; but he sold them to the vivisectionist. I answered the door to the man when he came, and pulled a frightful face at him; but he pushed past me and walked into Father's office and kicked the horse's hoof away so that the door shut. Later they came into the room where the animals were kept. I saw them looking at the yellow puppy with its laughing, panting face. It rolled over and played with the vivisectionist's pointed shoe. He offered my father a pound for it—and the kind tabby cat with its kittens, he paid another pound for the whole family; and Father was pleased and gave him a one-eyed rabbit as a makeweight.

When the man had driven away in his cart, with the animals all in sacks, my father put the money in his pigskin wallet and absent-mindedly chewed a pink, scented cachou. Then he told me to take a small dog over the river to Knightsbridge. I was glad to leave the house, but he made me wear a long white coat so that I resembled a veterinary assistant. I carried the little dog between the privet hedges, which were in flower and smelt sweet. The summer wind had blown paper bags about and they rustled between iron railings, and a very old man peered at us through a dirty window, looking as if the sun had never touched him and he had always been in that dark room. I came to a street of high warehouses where there were trams to take people across the river, and I boarded one and climbed upstairs because of the dog. The tide was out, and small boats near the bank were lying on their sides, and there was a lovely light everywhere.

I had to walk when we came to Fulham Road. The farther I went the more beautiful it became. The houses were mostly painted white or cream; and they had sunblinds and window-boxes filled with flowers. Children walked sedately beside elderly nannies who were pushing enormous prams. The prams had white canopies with fringes, and arranged on a frilly pillow would be a baby's flowering face. The shops here were so very large they didn't seem quite real to me. I could not imagine shopping in one, though other people evidently didn't feel this way because they were pouring in through doors opened by men with moustaches as large as my father's. The pavements were so wide there was room for everyone, and I felt shy in my white coat-overall among so many well-dressed women in their flowing dresses and long gloves. Pretty girls with fresh faces walked beside their elegant mothers, who were almost beautiful alone but beside their daughters resembled everlasting flowers that have lasted too long in the house all winter.

The small dog danced at the end of its lead when we crossed the road and came to a square of flat-faced houses. I delivered it to a grave-faced housekeeper, who took the little creature as if it were a parcel and shut the yellow door in my face. I stood outside in my absurd white overall and looked at the well-kept houses, the pretty square garden where ladies strolled under their parasols, and the flower-like babies asleep in their perambulators. Horses and carriages waited outside some houses, with liveried coachmen in attendance, and there were great motor-cars shining like fabulous monsters. It seemed to me that everything was rich and very safe—even the fat pigeon that was being stalked by a huge grey cat. I stood there in the sun and thought, 'Some day I'll have a baby with frilly pillows and men much grander than my father will open shop doors to me—both doors at once, perhaps.'

Chapter Two

ONCE A WEEK we were alone without my father. He would hire a trap from The Trumpet and drive about London to see sick animals, and would often bring them home with him. We liked these days. Sometimes Mother would sing the sad Welsh songs she used to sing when she was a girl, but lately she would say, "Alice dear, has he really gone? Do you think you could manage if I rest a little?" Then she would creep upstairs and lie under an old eiderdown filled with feathers from long-dead mountain hens, and have a warm brick to add extra comfort. I would take her cups of hot milk and tea; but she would eat nothing because she had pains that came and went. She seemed to like to be alone.

I would do the work and take the dogs as far as the arch to be excused. Sometimes I would run to Lucy's house for a few minutes and watch her sewing with her mother in their front room, with pins, paper patterns and material all round. It sometimes happened that the material they were sewing was beautiful and gleaming, or foamy; but usually it was heavy and dark. Lucy's mother did not like me to stay long in case Lucy stopped working to use her hands to speak to me, but Lucy would smile above her sewing and I knew by her gentle, greenish face she was glad I came.

One day, when I returned from seeing Lucy, I saw my father's hat in the hall and knew he was there. I always thought of him as wearing a top hat, but now I saw it was only one called a bowler. While I was looking at it, he came thundering out of his office with a thing like a large private rat under his arm. It turned out to be a mongoose. He kept shouting that he wanted his tea and where was Mother. He would have hit me if he hadn't been holding the mongoose. I escaped to the kitchen, but he came after me demanding a saucer of milk for the mongoose. He said it had got to live in the kitchen to make sure it was warm. I didn't welcome it, because I'd remembered hearing they eat live snakes.

When I was left alone with it, Mother came quietly down the stairs and into the kitchen. She was still doubled up with pain, but she said, "Don't tell him I've been lying down; I'll be better in a few minutes. What is that dreadful little animal? Have we got to have it in here?"

I just nodded as I fried fish for Father's tea. A

stronger kind of sadness than I usually knew suddenly came as I looked at Mother and saw how really ill she was. My heart was full of trouble as I rather awkwardly went to put my arm round her thin, sloping shoulders.

"No, no! don't leave the fish or it will burn," she whispered, "and don't forget to warm his plate. There, I'm better now. I'll make the tea."

We both bent over the gas oven as we listened to the sound of heavy feet pacing up and down the dining-room. Then his meal was ready and I took the tray in to him. He stood over me breathing deep, impatient breaths as I arranged the food on the table, and, when it was ready, he sat down and ate as if he were starving, although it was really earlier than he usually had his high tea. As he propped the evening paper up with the teapot, he said, "You know what you have to do with the animals in there," jerking his head in the direction of their room. "Well, get on with it and don't stand gaping at me."

I fed the animals and took the dogs to the red arch, and, when I returned, Mother was almost straight again and the pain had gone. We heard Father leave the house and it became a peaceful evening, except that we had a mongoose in the kitchen. A sudden rain came, and even the earth in our garden smelt good. Lucy had lent me a book called *Pomeroy Abbey* by Mrs.

Henry Wood. There was a ghost in it with a livid face and hare lip. I sat in a creaking chair made of basket and read until the daylight went and Mother lit the faintly hissing gas. I had to leave the ghost of the Lord of Pomeroy in the West Tower ("it has a dreadful look of reproach on its face") while we did our final work of laying morning trays, covering the parrot with an old flannel petticoat, and leaving ham in the dining-room for Father to eat when he came home in the night.

With a candle by my bed I read that the Lord of Pomeroy wasn't really a ghost but had shot the lower half of his brother's face right away. I was longing to know more, but heard Father return and knew that, when he had eaten the ham, he would pass my door, so the candle must go out.

I dreamt that I was walking with bare feet in a garden filled with snow, and above my head I carried an open parasol. Across a terrace, an almost square politician walked towards me. He came so near that our shoulders touched and sparks flashed from us. From the trees small cries and groans came, as if they were women in pain, and I thought, 'I did not cover the parrot with flannel,' and was awake in my bed.

The snow-covered garden had gone for ever, but the cries were still there.

In a long dressing-gown, made by Lucy from a

blanket, I stood on the landing to listen. The cries
were coming from Mother's room. They sounded
awful, and I wished I hadn't read about the Lord of
Pomeroy—perhaps the lower part of her face had been
shot away in the night. I went to her door, and,
although Mother was not religious any more, she was
crying to God and there was a light under her door.
Then I went in. Although her face was twisted with
pain and tear-drenched, it was all there. She lay with
her pain framed in the shining of her brass bed, and
she did not see me at first.

I called "Mother!" and she turned and saw me from
the sides of her eyes.

"Hush, dear, don't let your father know," she
whispered. "There is nothing you can do."

Although she protested that I might make a noise, I
filled her stone hot-water bottle with boiling water
and brought her a glass of warm milk; but there was
little I could do to help her and she lay there whimper-
ing. To my great relief she eventually dozed off. I
watched her in the gaslight. She lay all twisted under
the honeycomb counterpane. One hand kept moving,
but the rest of her was still. I felt a great sorrow for
her and knew that she would soon die, and that her
small and gentle presence would be gone and I would
be alone with Father. I did not like to leave her and
sat there until it was morning. On a wooden chair I

saw her little petticoat and rather grey and sad corsets waiting to be worn.

It was several days before the doctor came. It was my father who sent for him. Even he noticed something was wrong with Mother. When he saw her all doubled up over the dining-room sideboard, he suddenly bellowed, "For Christ's sake, woman, send for a doctor; and, if he can't put you right, keep out of my sight!"

She crept from the room, and I heard her climbing upstairs on all fours like an animal. It was somehow a terrible sound. Father stood listening and biting his moustache, and, when he heard her bedroom door close, he almost ran from the house. He returned quite soon and shut himself in his office, and a little later the doctor came.

He was a Jewish doctor who lived down the road. He was old and looked dirty, but he was kind. After he had examined Mother he went into the office and talked with Father, and I could hear from the kitchen that their voices were grave. Before he left, he called me out into the hall. He told me that Mother was dying and that all he could do to help her was to give her drugs to ease the pain. I was so grateful for the mention of pain-killing drugs that I caught hold of his hand and kept shaking it. He promised that a woman would come to help with nursing her and doing the housework. Then I went with him to his surgery to collect the medicines that were to relieve Mother's pain. The pavement was so hot from the sun I could feel it through my shoes. I'd forgotten it was summer outside.

It was the next day that Mrs. Churchill came. I opened the door to her and there she stood, old and square under her man's cloth cap, her legs very far apart and her stockings wrinkled. She spoke in a hoarse voice that was full of warm feeling.

"Yes, my dear," she croaked, "I've come to help you now your Ma's poorly. Is this the kitchen, ducks? Well I never, what a nice little rat!" She stroked the mongoose which was tied to a chair near the stove. Then she took off the cap, and I saw her hair was streaky red with pink combs in it. We went upstairs to my mother's room. It already seemed filled with illness and a smell of chlorodine sweets, but I noticed Mother was almost looking pretty, and I could imagine how she had looked when she was young. I could not have been looking after her very well because Mrs. Churchill croaked, "Oh! you poor creature. Let me make you comfortable," and flew at the bed and started taking it to pieces. Pillows were treated unmercifully and hot water was demanded for a blanket bath. I thought she was going to wash the blankets, but it was Mother who was washed.

Mrs. Churchill came to love Mother and she seemed fond of me and the animals; but she didn't like men. "Yer don't want to worry about them!" she would say with great scorn. If Father spoke to her, she would sniff in a sort of amused way and, as soon as his back was turned, mutter, "All right, all right, old moustaches." She was a great talker and used to stay hours longer than she was meant to. She would tell me about the people she had been in service with when she was a girl, and about her dogs. "Our house is all dogs' hairs and I like it that way: it feeds the carpets."

In spite of the dogs, she seemed to have a wonderful garden, its paths edged with broken china, all of beautiful colours. Over a cup of tea, she would dreamily tell me about every plant that grew in it. "Did I tell yer about the little old vine I've got that I grew from a pip?" Or "As true as I'm sitting here, my sunflower is twelve feet tall and still growing."

Chapter Three

AUTUMN CAME and Mother was still dying in her room. It was peaceful in there because Father was frightened of her illness and never visited her. Each Monday morning he would ask for her purse. I would hand it to him, all black and thin and worn. He would put in four sovereigns and four half-crowns, and the purse would come alive again. He could hardly bear to touch it and would wash his hands in the surgery afterwards. He made me take away Mother's out-door clothes, which hung on pegs in the hall; and the rather downtrodden slippers that lived under the kitchen dresser were thrown into the boiler as if they had been black beetles.

A young boy called Hank helped with the animals now because I had to do most of the cooking and all the shopping and see to Mother when Mrs. Churchill had gone home. In spite of the boy's help, I didn't look after Father as well as Mother used to, and he often hit me because the bacon was burnt or the coffee weak. Once, when I had ironed a shirt badly, he suddenly rushed at me like a charging bull in a thunderstorm, seeming to toss the shirt in some way with his head. I held on to the kitchen sink, too afraid to move. He came right up to me, and I saw the whites of his eyes were all red. He was only wearing his vest and trousers and was dreadfully hairy. He seized the arms of the shirt and was trying to tie them round my neck with his great square hands when the parrot suddenly started to give one of its awful laughs. Father seemed to go all limp, and stumbled from the room, while the parrot went on laughing.

This was the only time Father got really fierce all the time Mother was ill. On the whole, he was rather subdued and stayed in the house as little as possible. He never asked after Mother. Sometimes the doctor would catch him in the hall, and then he would have to listen to him; but usually, when the doctor came, he would go out.

One morning a dreadful thing happened. A man came to measure Mother for her coffin as if she were dead already. He said Father had told him to come. Mrs. Churchill sent him away, but Mother kept calling, "Who was that? Who was that?" and we had to make excuses. In the afternoon she seemed worse, and whimpered and moaned and would not be comforted. The people waiting with their dogs and cats in the hall could hear her. It was like some awful symphony—Mother's sad sounds, and the screams and laughs of the parrot, and the howls and barks of the dogs, and in the background a plaintive chorus of mews from the cats. Father came out of the surgery, grey in the face, and hissed in my ear, "Keep her quiet! I won't have that noise. I can't stand it, I tell you!"

I went upstairs to Mother's room, where Mrs. Churchill was fanning her with a newspaper. The autumn sun streamed through a gap in the curtains, and I could see that Mother's face was wet with tears of pain although her eyes were closed. I felt desperate to help her, but there was nothing I could do. She had had her medicine and the doctor had visited her already that day.

"Oh, Mrs. Churchill, what can we do?" I cried in despair.

She gave me a comforting tap with the newspaper, and said, "Don't take on, lovey. Why don't yer get the old doctor round again? He might give her a bit of something extra to ease her."

I ran from the house and the relief was so great to be outside, away from Mother's pain. The first autumn leaves were on the pavements, very yellow and not yet dry. Pale Michaelmas daisies showed through iron railings, but there were early pink chrysanthemums in the doctor's garden and they smelt bitter and wintery. I pulled the bell. It hung on a chain and had a handle with PULL written on it as if it were a lavatory plug, and I thought perhaps this was intentional as it was a doctor's house. The doctor answered the door himself. He was already wearing his dark coat, and the sun on his face showed how old and tired he was. He blinked at me for a moment and then said, "Mother not so well? That's a pity, poor thing," and he took me into the hall. "I'll just get a little something to help her. Wait there, my dear." He pointed to a little wooden chair with the seat shaped like a shield and something carved in it. His hall was much larger than ours and the floor was made of many-coloured tiles. There was a bead curtain to hide the part of the hall that led to the kitchen. I was fascinated by a hall-stand carved with heads of lions that had rings in their mouths, but before I could look long the doctor came trotting out of his surgery and we left the house together.

The people with their dogs and cats had left our house and Father had gone, too; but the parrot greeted us with its shrill cries and little Hank stumped past us carrying a basket of dirty straw. There were no sounds from Mother's room and when we went upstairs we saw she was half asleep, although one hand kept twitching on the counterpane. The doctor looked down at her pinched little face, still wet with tears, then opened his case and injected her arm with something. He gave me a box of tablets which were only to be used when she seemed in great pain. He said she would sleep soundly for an hour or two—already her hand was quite still.

"Why don't you get her a few flowers and fruit? Ladies like little attentions when they are ill." He looked round her dreary room and the sagging brass bed, and, although I could do nothing about the room, I was ashamed about the flowers. I could have bought them, but it had never occurred to me—no one ever gave Mother flowers. And, of course, she should have had grapes. Ill people in books always had grapes or peaches beside their bed. As soon as the doctor left the house, I looked at the black purse. It had not gone all thin and flat yet; so I rushed to the market where the stalls were blazing with flowers and fruit. It was such a change to buy beautiful things instead of the usual 'pussy's pieces' and everlasting cabbage.

Mrs. Churchill had gone and I was alone with Mother when she woke from her deep sleep. When she saw her water jug filled with golden-rod, she just stared in amazement.

"Did your father put them there?" she asked. When I told her they were bought on the doctor's orders, she looked disappointed. Then she saw the purple grapes in a little round wicker basket and was quite be-wildered. "Are these doctor's orders, too?" she asked. "I hope your father won't be cross."

Father did not come home so I was able to have tea with Mother. I found a crochet cloth to put on her tray and cut the bread and butter very thin and I could tell she was pleased. She seemed to be quite free from pain and, although she was rather dreamy, better than she had been for weeks. She didn't eat the grapes but she kept looking at the golden-rod as longingly as if she would like to eat that instead.

"Golden-rod grew quite wild at the farm. And Michaelmas daisies, too—deep purple they were, not like the miserable little London ones you see about here. It's sour, the soil in London, and so is the life I've led. Oh, Alice, you have missed so much here! I had such a happy girlhood on the farm. The work was hard, but it was good rewarding work; and the pleasure it was to find an unexpected nest of eggs in some strange place. Early in the year there would be the lambs in the kitchen. How they used to tug at the bottle! And it was my job to feed them. I used to make the butter, too, and read a book while I churned. Suddenly the noise in the churn would change, just when my arm was aching unbearably, and I'd know the butter was coming. Under the trees round the farm there was the greenest moss, and in the summer and sometimes when it was raining I'd take off my boots and walk on it barefooted. There was no road to the farm, but we used the little railway track that belonged to the slate mines up the mountain. It was my work to get the sheep off the track when I could hear a truck coming down."

She turned away from the golden-rod and caught my hand in her own little pussy's paw of a hand and cried, "Dear Alice, I don't want to leave you here alone with him. I would write home and ask them to have you, but they are all gone now. Father and Mother died soon after you were born. It was the snow that killed Father. Rescuing the ewes and their lambs in the deep snow, he fell and was injured on the rocks below. He died a few days later. I longed to go home and comfort Mother, but your father wouldn't allow it; and, when she died from some internal complaint a few months later, he quarrelled with my brothers over the inheritance. There was only the farm and it was right and proper that my brothers should have it. Already I'd had a hundred pounds that my granny had left me. That was my dowry. I think it was the dowry that made your father ask for me. There was Evans the Post wanting me, too. He'd have been glad to have me without the money, but my parents wouldn't consider it. But when Euan Rows-lands, the veterinary with the royal blood of the Cadwalladers in his veins, came asking for me, they thought it a fine thing. He was a great and clever young man, but I was always afraid of him. When we were walking in the heather on such a grand and happy day you could hear all the insects humming, he suddenly began telling me about a tortoise and how he had severed the poor thing's head off its body when it was alive. Part of an experiment, he said, but it was a cruel thing to do. Farm life is often hard on animals, but not cruel like that."

She lay deep in the pillows and closed her eyes for a few minutes; it seemed she was sleeping, but she opened her sad stone eyes again and went on, "I would have liked to have called our marriage off but did not wish to disappoint my parents. We were married in the spring—on St. David's day. The chapel was decorated with leeks and daffodils. I'll always remember the overpowering smell of the leeks and I've never had them in the house since. I don't think your father fancies them either. We had some rooms over a shop in Blaenau-Ffestiniog, a grey, slaty place, but I was happy enough in a way. There was a tap and a yellow sink in the kitchen—I'd never seen water come out of a tap before, and turned it on a hundred times a day. Your father was just an assistant then to Davis the veterinary—and how he used to complain when old Davis took the horse and he had to walk! He made me unlace his boots when he came home and I remember he once kicked me in the face, he was in such a rage, and broke my front teeth. He was sorry afterwards and the next day he bought me a big fur muff, but I didn't like having crooked teeth and having to tell people I'd fallen down the stairs or some such talk. I'd have rather been without the muff and had straight teeth."

She ran a finger over her poor broken teeth, then continued, "Did I tell you about little Miss Thomas who was always sending for your father to see to her Dandie Dinmonts? They were queer little dogs with silver fur like smoke upon their heads and I haven't seen any like them since. She wouldn't have old Davis near the dogs; it always had to be your father. And then he started going round there in the evenings and they would play cards together; so there I was alone with only the water-tap for company, and you couldn't spend all the evening turning the water on and off. The farm was nearly ten miles away and I couldn't walk there and back the same night. I would sit alone, remembering how my brothers would take me along with them in the evenings to the post office. It was the great meeting-place of the village and we would all sit on benches and talk and sing; and the men talked politics and we girls talked about the little things we were putting aside for our weddings—even the girls who had not yet a lover, they were putting by, too. Sometimes the Minister would join us and the talk would turn to parish matters and we would end the evening singing hymns; and, although my voice was thin and small, I did so love to sing. My brothers used to tease me and call me the singing mouse.

"One evening, when I couldn't bear the lonely sadness any longer, I went round to Miss Thomas's little villa on the outskirts of the town. Through the lace curtains of the parlour I could see them, Euan and Miss Thomas. There was your father sitting back in an easy chair, smoking a cigar and looking as if it was his own home; and Miss Thomas was tinkling away on her piano, with the candles burning away in the holders. And there I was in the front garden looking through the window like a Peeping Tom. Already at that time I was carrying you and it was a sad thing to do, watching my husband sitting in another woman's parlour all at home like that. He was even wearing slippers all coloured with embroidery, slippers I'd never seen—doubtless they had been worked by Miss Thomas herself. One thing I must say: although he was pretty comfortable, he looked fed up with Miss Thomas's fussy little way of playing the piano. Although she crossed her hands when she played 'The Maiden's Prayer', it wasn't real music. As I looked at her, I couldn't help thinking how like an old hen only fit for boiling she looked, a plucked, rather yellow old hen; her neck was scrawny as if it had already been wrung. I stood at the window watching them through the lace curtains. Suddenly Miss Thomas glanced at the window and said something to your father and, jumping from the music-stool, she skipped across the room to draw the curtains. So all I saw was pink curtains with a light glowing through.

"I never saw Miss Thomas again. It was only a week or two later that she was killed in the street by a runaway horse-and-dray carrying barrels of beer. It wasn't the horse that killed her but one of the barrels: it rolled off and completely crushed her. She was a little wisp of a woman and a barrel of beer was too much for her. Poor thing! she was a member of the Temperance Society, too, and they all clubbed together and sent her a beautiful wreath of violets woven into a harp."

Mother paused and I knew she was thinking of death which was so close beside her now, and I think we were both hoping she would be allowed a wreath or two. Then she went on:

"I think I've told you before, Alice, that it was Miss Thomas's money that enabled your father to buy this house and practice. She left everything to him. It caused rather a scandal at the time. People in Blaenau didn't like it at all; but they couldn't take the money away. The will was proved and it was all in order, and then your father's one idea was to get to London. I think it was a mistaken one and the London he imagined was a mistaken one, too. He'd just been through it the once in a cab from Victoria Station to Paddington, and he must have been driven in a round-about way (no doubt the cabby wanted a good fare) because he saw Buckingham Palace and St. James's and Piccadilly and Oxford Street and the Edgware Road. He thought all London was like that—big houses and wide streets and, if there were slums, they were some-where near the docks. He advertised for a veterinary practice and when he had a reply from a gentleman with a flourishing practice on the borders of Clapham and Battersea, he thought it sounded a fine thing. The price seemed very reasonable, the house and all included. A commodious, well-furnished house it was called, and Euan thought there would be big pillars in front and a fine flight of steps leading to a handsome front door. I remember we arrived at Euston Station and I thought it must be raining, it was so dark; but, as we left the station, I saw the sky was a yellowish-black. I'd never seen one like it before. It was the yellow that horrified me. At first the streets were so small and mean Euan thought we had got out at the wrong station and it wasn't London at all. Then we came to some better streets, but we didn't see a palace, only some large furniture shops. After the furniture shops things got better—until we crossed the river.

"The river was a surprise to me: it was so wide, dirty, and busy with boats. There was one great black hulk of a boat moored near the bridge, and standing up in it were old tombstones and crosses. A kind of floating graveyard, it seemed to be, only the tombstones were too close together to give comfort to the dead.

"Then we came to the poor streets, mean and narrow. Euan sat in the cab slumped up and the pride all gone from him and I dared not speak. It seemed a long time before we came to a steep hill. I began to think it would be better when we reached the top, but we turned away down a side-street and, when we had passed under the railway arch, we were in Glenmore Terrace. Oh! your father was disappointed with the house; it wasn't at all what he expected. Poor man! he just trailed about from room to room, and there was disappointment for him everywhere. But he turned to me, for that little time he turned to me, until he got the practice going, and then he had other interests. I expect I was a disappointment, too. . . ."

Her voice trailed away as if it were vanishing down a passage, then suddenly returned:

"It was when we first came here that the photograph

was taken. Your father didn't want them to know at home that things had turned out badly for him, so thought it a good idea to send a photograph of us looking like high life, and it really was a lovely picture. I've put it away now because it saddens me; but I'd like you to have it, Alice. There we are sitting in a theatre box with draped curtains all tasselled, and Euan is wearing a velvet smoking-jacket and bow tie, and my hair is all fluffed out and I've a little pair of opera glasses in my hand. It was the sweetest photograph, but, of course, it wasn't a real box: it was just built in the studio and you had to climb steps to get to it. I think it was sometimes used as a pulpit for the clergy to be photographed in, because there was a Prayer Book which could be used instead of the opera glasses."

I thought Mother had gone to sleep until she started talking about the mountains

"I've missed them so much all these years, the hills and mountains. The sun would disappear behind them so suddenly, and the clouds would become entangled in their peaks. Some are dark and furry with trees; and other more rocky ones are covered in heather filled with singing insects in summer; and there are the ones I used to call book mountains, just made of flat lumps of slate, like piles of giant's grey books. Dark brown moss grew in the mere by the farm; and once

I saw a little child floating on the surface. She was dead, but I wasn't afraid because she looked so pure floating there, with her eyes open and her blue pinafore gently moving. It was Flora, a little girl who had been missing for three days . . . Little Miss Thomas had a china bowl on her window-sill; it was filled with large glass allies of all colours . . . strange things for a spinster lady to own, but . . . I saw them. . . ."

Chapter Four

AN INDIAN WEARING A TURBAN came for the mongoose and took it away under his coat. The kitchen kept much cleaner without it: I didn't kick saucers of milk across the floor when I was in a hurry. The Indian gave me a bottle of scent because he thought I'd been kind to his mongoose; but I hadn't, so I gave it to Mrs. Churchill, who had really liked the little creature. She liked the scent, too, which was a good thing because Father had hurt her feelings and called her 'a filthy old hag' when he found her polishing his surgery floor with her cloth cap on the end of a mop.

The flowers were still alive in Mother's room, and she lay there, quite quiet, looking at them. She had talked so much the previous evening that she was exhausted, too tired even to eat her grapes, though I think she liked to know they were there. The doctor came and, when he was leaving, managed to catch Father in the hall. They went into the dining-room together, and I could hear their rumbling voices as I prepared the animals' meat in the kitchen. Little Hank came for the bowls, one by one. He was a very under-sized boy, perhaps because he did not have sufficient food. His mother was a poor Dutch widow who had somehow become stranded in Clapham, and Hank was the eldest of a family of five boys. Often I would find him munching dog biscuits behind the door, and once a raw herring. Sometimes his mother would pass our house and I'd see her with her hat on the back of her untidy head and all the little boys, who seemed to be wearing boots much too large, clattering after her. I think they must have worn iron heels because they sounded rather like little horses.

Lucy came round in the afternoon. She said her mother had sent her out because her eyes ached so much from sewing mourning clothes in a great hurry. She rather sadly said with her hands, "I don't want to lose my eyesight as well as hearing and speaking." But she cheered up over our tea in the kitchen and told me she was going to be a dressmaker apprentice in a large shop in Bayswater. "You see, Mother is giving up the dressmaking and it will be a wonderful chance for me. They even make Court gowns." Then she produced a fortune-telling tape-measure and we laughed a lot over it. My waist measurement said, 'Next year', and my wrist 'He loves you', and my nose 'A sailor', and my head 'You will be surprised'. We were still laughing when I heard Father come in and I knew our happy time was over and I would have to get Lucy out of the house quickly. I heard him go into the surgery, and that gave Lucy a chance to escape. As we passed through the hall we saw his black leather case on the table. Sometimes brown would show through the black and Mother would polish it with black boot-polish. If any got on the handles there was trouble, because it came on Father's gloves, which were often meant to be yellow.

Lucy had gone when Father came out of the surgery. Instead of coming to the kitchen to demand tea he went upstairs and, to my amazement, into Mother's room. It was the first time he had been there since she became ill. I could hardly believe it. I stood at the bottom of the stairs and could hear their voices. I thought I heard her say, "It's not right. Oh, Euan!" Then later, "Please be kind to Alice. It would be best to send her away from here." Father wasn't shouting or in a temper—in fact, his voice was very quiet—so I returned to the kitchen and grilled two chops and two tomatoes cut in half, real English ones. I could tell they were English because the little green piece you pull off smelt fresh and tomatoey.

Father came downstairs and went into his surgery. Although he could smell food cooking, he left the house almost immediately. Later I went up to Mother, but she was asleep, just a mound in her brass bed. The house was quiet. Even the animals were still, and I almost wished the parrot would start his dreadful laughter. Father didn't return and Mother still slept. Her breathing became heavy. I kept imagining I could hear it in other rooms and wished Mrs. Churchill were there to tell me about her flowers. "A great striped dahlia, dear, twelve inches across—and there are nine buds to come. Did I tell you about my early chrysanthemums that I grew from cuttings a park-keeper let me have?" she would say dreamily over a cup of mahogany tea; and I would stare at her pink haircombs, half-hypnotised and strangely comforted. There was no Mrs. Churchill to comfort me, but, when I took the dogs to lift their legs on the red arch, it seemed better because I met people walking up the hill. In one gas lamp there were some crickets chirping, or there may have been something wrong with the gas, but I hoped it was crickets. When I turned into our road, I thought I saw a figure waving from the doorstep and I was afraid again in case it was something terrible. It twisted and turned like some dreadful shadow. I called, "I'm coming"; but it went on twisting and turning, and my legs wouldn't walk properly. Then, when I was near, I saw it was really a shadow from a large flag that someone had nailed to a post in their garden and was fluttering and waving in the night.

I went into the house and put the three dogs in their cages. Usually they whined at first, but this evening they quietly settled down on their straw and curled up neatly. An old white cock with a swollen eye pushed his head through the bars of his pen, and I gave him a few grains of Indian corn which he pecked from my hand. He was a child's pet and very tame for a cock— much tamer than the parrot, who nipped and pecked me on every occasion. Then I covered the parrot up with the flannel petticoat. There were only the trays to lay for the morning, but I lingered over the animals because I didn't want the house to be filled with breathing.

As I climbed upstairs I could hear the breathing again, now that everything in the house was still. I went to Mother's room and she was still asleep. Her face was flushed, and her breathing was certainly very loud. Although it seemed cruel, I shook her; but she still stayed asleep and the heavy breathing seemed to come louder. I didn't know if it was a good thing, all this heavy-breathing sleep, or if I should send for the doctor although it was so late at night. I even wished Father would come home and tell me what to do. Eventually I left her well propped up with pillows so that she would not suffocate and went to bed. Even with the door closed the sound of breathing seemed to be there.

I was so tired I slept nearly as soundly as Mother, but a rattling, snoring sound seemed to come in my dreams. Suddenly I was awake and knew it had stopped, and everywhere was very silent. Then I heard Father return and creep up to his room, although the night had nearly gone and light was coming.

The next time I woke up it was quite late in the morning and I realised I'd overslept. Already I could hear Father's voice, and there seemed to be several people creeping about the stairs. When I was half-dressed, I opened my door a chink. I saw a strange woman with an enamel jug of water in her hand. She went into Mother's room and firmly closed the door. When I was dressed I went downstairs expecting great trouble to come because I hadn't taken Father's breakfast up to his room. Already he was down in the dining-room talking to someone. As I passed the room, the door was suddenly opened by the little old doctor. He beckoned to me with his yellow, wrinkled hand and said, "Come here, missy, I want you."

I went in and the morning sun was making a Jacob's ladder right across the room. Father was leaning on the mantelpiece with his back to me, and his clothes, which usually looked so fine and smooth, were all wrinkled as if he had slept in them. The doctor

37

started asking me questions. Had I given Mother any of the pills that were to relieve her pain? Exactly what had she had to eat and drink after his visit yesterday? When had I last seen her and how had she seemed? I answered the first questions, but, when it came to the third question, I started to cry and said I knew now I should have sent for him. I tried to explain my confused feelings and how I had not known what to do for the best. I told him about the breathing, and how I was not sure if I could really hear it or imagined it because I was afraid. I told him how I'd propped Mother up with pillows and tried to wake her. "But she hasn't suffocated?" I wailed. "Please don't say she has suffocated. I saw a strange woman with hot water: surely she wouldn't need hot water if she had suffocated?"

It was then that the doctor told me that Mother had died in her sleep and there was nothing I could have done to save her. He kept patting me with his old wrinkled hands, and tried to bring comfort by telling me how much she would have suffered if she had lived the last two or three weeks, which was the most she could have lasted.

As I stumbled from the room a dreadful thought came and filled me with horror. Perhaps Father had given Mother something to put her to sleep, just as he put the animals to sleep that the vivisectionist did not need for his experiments. Mother really had gone to sleep, but the animals were given poison on their tongues, although he called it 'putting them to sleep'.

During the morning a man came to measure Mother for her coffin. It was the same man we had sent away two days before.

Chapter Five

THEY BURIED MOTHER three days later, and she had a wreath on her coffin made of white chrysanthemums. Mrs. Churchill bought a beautiful glass dome of flowers called 'Immortals', which would last for ever on Mother's grave unless "those dratted boys broke it with stones". Father attended the funeral, and then he went away. A locum came to look after the practice. He was a young, healthy-looking man with a happy, hairy face, and his body somehow looked rather like a tree-trunk. He blinked his large, almost round, blue eyes and to myself I called him Blinkers, but his real name was Henry Peebles. He was the first man who had ever treated me with politeness and consideration. I noticed this, but it did not mean much to me at the time because I was feeling so sad and lost and kindness almost made it worse.

Blinkers looked after the animals with Hank's help and Mrs. Churchill managed the house and meals; so there was only the shopping left for me to do. Mrs.

Churchill would tell me what to buy and Father had put quite a lot of money in Mother's old purse before he went away.

I think it must have been the first time I'd ever had time on my hands. I wandered round the streets of Clapham and Battersea in a dreary kind of dream. I remember looking in the windows of a number of outsize women's shops from which smirking, comely matrons, wearing shapeless dresses, gazed back at me with glass eyes. I walked on Clapham Common, where already autumn bonfires were burning although the leaves had hardly begun to fall, and ice-cream cornets were still being sold. I awoke from my dreary dream to listen to the speech-makers. I couldn't understand what they were talking about, but gathered they were mostly angry about something. I listened to the Salvation Army band, and somehow felt afraid of them. Terrible thoughts about Father putting Mother to sleep came into my mind, and I felt I might start shouting them out loud to the music.

I found a beautiful and peaceful church in Battersea by the river. I think it was called St. Mary's. I wasn't afraid there. It had only a small churchyard, but I liked to sit in it and watch the barges and hear the river sounds. Sometimes barges were moored to the churchyard walls, and savoury smells of cooking came in the autumn air. I liked Battersea Park better than

Clapham Common because there were more flowers and I often discovered new parts I never knew existed before. I found a dear little imitation river, with wild banks.

I must have walked miles those first few weeks after Mother died, but I couldn't bear to be home and always thinking of her.

Everywhere in the house there were sad little reminders—a limp string shopping-bag hanging from the kitchen door; a fortune-telling book in the dresser-drawer; a fern in the dining-room window that had died from neglect since she had ceased to tend it; and one small black glove mixed up with the string she used to save—little things like that were everywhere.

I had not been in her bedroom since she died. Mrs. Churchill had cleaned it and said it was to be kept locked until Father returned. "He'll want to go through her things," she said in a hoarse whisper; and she locked the door and put the key on Father's organ-like desk.

There was a bachelor blackbird who lived in the dusty holly tree in the front garden. Mother had been so fond of him. Every spring he had sung madly, hoping to attract a mate, but one had never come and Mother had fussed and worried over him and would say exasperatedly, "If only he would leave that wretched holly bush and fly to the Common, he'd soon find a wife. He can't expect a bird to want to nest in a bed of dirty holly." The blackbird still sang in the holly bush, but Mother had gone.

At night I was all alone in the house. Although I slept with my head under the bedclothes, I could hear awful creakings on the stairs, and sometimes I thought I could hear whispering by my bed. I asked Mrs. Churchill if she would stay and keep me company; but she said her husband didn't like her to be out at night, and she had 'our Vera's' boy staying with her while his mother was in hospital. One night the dogs started barking and yelping and I thought something terrible really had happened. I lay in bed shivering, too afraid to go and see if the house were on fire, or if burglars were creeping through the pantry window. In the morning I found the cage that contained the old cock with the diseased eye had fallen to the ground, and the poor bird was dead and heavy.

Three weeks after Mother's funeral, Father came home.

Chapter Six

FATHER ARRIVED IN THE AFTERNOON, and he wasn't alone. A tall, fair-haired woman was with him. When she smiled, she rolled her eyes. Father said, "This is Miss Fisher—Rosa Fisher, and she has come here to be my housekeeper and you will find her a great help. I suppose Mrs. Churchill is still here? Well, tell her to get Miss Fisher a room ready."

The cab-driver dumped the last of the luggage in the hall, and Father paid him and slammed the front door just as a German band started playing 'Land of Hope and Glory' in front of the house. He went into the surgery and I was left with Miss Fisher. Above the din, she said, "I'm so pleased to meet you, dear. Your dear father has been telling me about you. He talks a lot about his little girl." She made mouths and grimaces as she talked, and her accent was so affected it was difficult to hear what she was saying. "Do you think I could go up to my little room, dear, and take my things off? It doesn't matter if it

44

isn't ready. I don't know if you were expecting me."

"No," I told her. "I wasn't expecting you."

We went upstairs and passed my room. I was determined she shouldn't have that, and she couldn't have Mother's room, all locked up as it was; and Father wouldn't want her in his fine big bedroom. So there was only the little room that belonged to the sewing-machine and the dressmaker's dummy. I opened the door and saw it was half-filled with trunks and boxes and very dusty. There was a small bed in a corner, with a thin mattress rolled up like a sausage, and there were a few chairs and a table; but there was nowhere to put clothes. Miss Fisher gave a start when she saw the room, then she uttered a little cry and one hand flew to her breast.

"My God, that figure! It gave me quite a shock for the moment." She looked at the room with great distaste, and said, "I can't quite picture myself sleeping in a room like this. I shall speak to your father about it. I'd like to see your little room, if I may, dear."

I refused to show it to her, and ran downstairs to find Mrs. Churchill and ask her advice.

Mrs. Churchill was collecting tea-things from the dresser, her square back turned to the door and her legs so far apart I suddenly thought they might be fixed on the outside of her body as dolls' legs often are. She wheeled round when I spoke to her, and I could see she had great news to impart.

"Do yer know who that is?" she croaked. "It's Rosa from The Trumpet—her that waits in the dining-room and helps in the bar sometimes. Housekeeper, my foot! She's a strumpet if ever there was one."

I told Mrs. Churchill about there being no suitable room for the strumpet from The Trumpet, and how she seemed to have her eye on mine. "I'd lock it if I could, but there isn't a key," I said bitterly. Then we listened and heard her opening all the doors, including mine, at least, all the doors except Mother's, because that was still locked. Then she came downstairs and went into the surgery to Father, who was talking to the locum. We distinctly heard him say, "Go away, can't you see I'm busy? Make yourself some tea or something." And when she came into the kitchen her affectations had temporarily deserted her and she was just a long, thin woman who was feeling rather lost and snubbed. She took off her hat and stood in the kitchen doorway, fingering the artificial cherries it was decorated with. Later, I discovered they were filled with cotton-wool, because I took one to pieces the first time Miss Fisher left the house without her cherry-trimmed hat.

She stood in the door looking down at her hat, and

Mrs. Churchill demanded, "Now, Rosa Fisher, what are you doing here?"

"It's none of your business if Mr. Rowlands wants me to be his housekeeper, poor widower that he is."

"Poor widower, my foot! Mrs. Rowlands would turn in her grave if she knew the likes of you was in her house. You just hop it back to The Trumpet, where you belong."

Mrs. Churchill stumped to the gas stove and lit a jet under the kettle, which somehow made the kitchen seem to belong to her, and Miss Fisher went out, shouting, "You'll be the one to regret this. You'll be slung out on your ear, you old bulldog!"

Father came out of the surgery and they both went into the dining-room together. Then they went upstairs and I heard Father say, "It doesn't matter which room you have because you won't be using it much. Eh, Rosa?" When they came downstairs, he told me I was to make some tea and boil some fresh eggs. "And you can show Miss Fisher the kitchen and tell her anything she wants to know." He nodded his head at Mrs. Churchill and jerked his thumb over his shoulder, and as they left the kitchen together I saw she was rolling up her sleeves as if she were going to fight Father, but, when she came back, she was crying. Fortunately, Miss Fisher was already in the dining-room, sitting behind the best china teapot, waiting for Father.

Father had given Mrs. Churchill a week's notice. We sat over our tea discussing it in low voices. "It's the ingratitude of it that gets me. After all I've done for your ma. If it wasn't for leaving you with that trollop, I'd leave the house for good this night."

"Oh, Mrs. Churchill, don't leave me alone with them straight away!" I wailed. "She may be gone in a week, and we could continue as we were before; and you could go on telling me about your garden and your daughter's boy, and we'd soon forget about Miss Fisher."

"My! that reminds me, there's 'er room to get ready. She's going to 'ave yer ma's room, but it's going to be all done up and we've got to take out all yer ma's stuff and put it in the box-room. It don't seem right, all her poor things treated like that."

We started clearing Mother's room that evening, and it saddened me to see her limp little clothes hanging in the wardrobe. I'd forgotten how small Mother was. One thing, they were much too small for Miss Fisher to wear—it would have been terrible to see her in Mother's clothes. There was the muff Father gave her when they were first married. It smelt of old bears now. There were several pairs of pointed black boots with buttons on the side and worn slippers with big buckles, and an old sealskin coat that had belonged to her mother. As we piled all her things on to the box-room bed, we heard Father taking Rosa Fisher out for the evening, and Mrs. Churchill said, "House-keeper, be damned!"

Mrs. Churchill made up the bed and went home, and I stayed in Mother's room emptying the contents of the drawers into large cardboard boxes and a thing called a Gladstone bag. I struck a match and lit the gas and in the greenish light there were her combinations, camisoles and petticoats that would not be needed any more, all sorrowful and limp; in the brass bed where she had suffered so much Miss Fisher would lie rolling her eyes. The little drawers at the top were filled with so many small things Mother had treasured —white kid gloves that looked as if they had never been worn and faded photographs of her family; a Prayer Book with a white celluloid cover, and a box decorated with shells—the box had a pin-cushion in the centre, and inside there were a few pieces of jewellery, brooches filled with hair, large silver lockets that had once contained photographs, and a small gold heart filled with dried heather. I arranged the photographs in the shell box with the jewellery and put them away in my room. Then I found the photograph of Mother and Father all dressed up in the imitation theatre box—Mother looking so pretty and gentle, and Father so upright and grand. It seemed terrible to think that it was only taken about sixteen years ago. I tried to remember if I'd ever heard them talking together as ordinary people seemed to, but I couldn't; I couldn't even remember them leaving the house together. Sometimes when I was a child Mother had taken me to the country or Wimbledon Common for a few hours, but Father never came with us. He treated Mother as if she was contemptible and completely ignored me. As a young child, I'd always been kept out of his way and the only meal we ever had together was our midday dinner. Mother once said that, if I'd been a boy, it might have been different. But, when I think of him kicking Mother's front teeth crooked so early in their marriage, it really was a mercy he ignored me, or I might have had a cauliflower ear, or something equally disfiguring.

Poor Mother! I took the last of her things into the box-room and went to bed; but just as I was starting to dream, Father and Rosa Fisher returned. I think they must have been to a music-hall, because she was singing a song and laughing at the same time, and I even thought I heard Father laugh. As they passed my door, she said, "We mustn't wake up the little girl." Then she seemed to stand outside for a moment, and I heard her exclaim, "Here, you said she was a bit simple. She seems all there, a bit too much all there for me." "Oh! you don't want to worry yourself about her," came the answer, "she does what she's told." And then they made a kind of scuffling noise and Rosa started to giggle and they went together into Father's room. In the morning she was in her own room because she called to me and asked for a cup of tea. When I took it, I said, "Wouldn't you rather have it in Father's room?" "No, he's dressing now," she yawned. "Hey! what do you mean, you cheeky little bitch?"

I ran down to the kitchen and suddenly felt terribly dirty and miserable, although I'd washed that morning. I'd somehow known Father and Rosa Fisher would sleep together from the way Mrs. Churchill had talked, and I knew there was something dirty and bad about it. But I felt ashamed of myself for referring to it in such a pert and cheeky way. In future I'd ignore it and try not to think about it and certainly not mention it.

As I was washing the tears from my face, I heard the front door-bell and guessed it was Mr. Peebles, the locum. I hoped he wouldn't see that I'd been crying, but, if he did, he was still as polite and respectful as ever, and beamed at me with his kind, happy face. I gave him a cup of rather stewed tea and we talked in the kitchen for a few minutes, but, just when we were laughing together I remembered Father's breakfast.

Mr. Peebles offered to help, but I sent him away to the animals. I felt much better now I'd laughed and talked a little with someone who was kind.

Decorators came, and Mother's room became all pink, and there were curtains with roses on them, and the wash-basin and jug had roses on them, too. I thought how Mother would have loved it; but it was as if she had never been. It was called Miss Fisher's room now.

It was terrible having Rosa Fisher and Mrs. Churchill in the house together because they quarrelled all the time. Although I was fond of Mrs. Churchill, I was glad when she went and the insults that had been shouted from room to room, and the almost frightful silences, at last came to an end. When she left, she had tears in her eyes. She gave me her address, written in pencil on a mauve envelope, in case I ever needed her help—"because, my poor little dear, you don't seem to 'ave a friend in the world."

But Mrs. Churchill was not the only friend I had. Mr. Peebles became my friend, too. He told me he'd like to be one the day he was leaving. I thought he was just being polite, but a few days later there he was on the doorstep asking me to go driving with him the following Sunday, and although I knew Father would half kill me if he found out, I agreed to go. We arranged to meet outside The Trumpet because that was where the pony and trap were to be hired; but when he had gone, I wished we hadn't chosen such a public place. In fact, I was terrified every time I thought about Sunday. The days seemed to pass much quicker than usual, and it was Sunday very soon.

It was a bright October day and nearly as warm as summer and everything seemed to go my way. No one noticed I put the kitchen clock on a quarter of an hour so that I could get the midday dinner over early. Rosa Fisher helped me a little in the kitchen, but she spent most of the morning sitting on the table reading the *News of the World*, and, as soon as our meal was finished, took it up to her pink room to read while she had a rest. I only washed up a few things, and hid the rest in the oven and crept up to my bedroom to change my clothes. Lucy's mother had made me a black serge dress when Mother died, and there was a little black jacket that went with it. It was rather a sombre outfit, but the cut and fit was really very good and it showed off my pale yellow hair. I dressed very carefully and went downstairs, but as I passed the dining-room door Father shouted "Alice!" and I thought my lovely afternoon was going to be taken away. I put my head just round the door so that he couldn't see I was all dressed up. He was sitting in the leather arm-chair, looking terribly morose and not doing anything at all except bite his moustache and look out of the window at the dirty holly tree. I was going to slip away again because he seemed to have forgotten me, but he slowly turned his head and said in a heavy, flat voice, "Where are you going?" The only thing I could do was lie, so I crossed my fingers (because it isn't supposed to matter so much if you do that) and said, "Only for a walk—with Lucy, I expect, that is, if she is in." He turned his eyes to the window again and muttered something about being back at four-thirty to get tea. Then he suddenly swung round on me and shouted, "I don't care what the hell you do, get out of here!"

I went. I ran from the house and almost danced through the streets. When I came to The Trumpet, the trap was already outside and Mr. Peebles was talking to the groom. He helped me into the trap and wrapped me round with a rug, although it was so warm, and then we went driving towards Wimbledon Common. I could look down on to people's heads, and in front there was the horse's nice round behind with a beautiful long black tail flowing down the middle. We went so fast that I had to hold my hat on my head, and it reminded me of the time, years ago, when I had a ride on the roundabouts. I'd been in closed cabs and trams before, but never in an open trap, and I kept telling Mr. Peebles how lovely it was. Then I suddenly became shy of him because I didn't

think it was right to show so much pleasure to someone who was almost a stranger. So we drove along in
silence; but we were still both happy.

When we came to the Common, we drove to the
windmill, left the trap there and had our tea on a
woody slope near. Mr. Pebbles had been to great
trouble preparing tea. He'd brought sandwiches with
cucumber inside, and little iced cakes, and a kettle and
a spirit stove. When I saw the kettle I rather wanted
to make a bonfire to boil it over, but he said it wasn't
allowed. So we used methylated spirits instead and no
laws were broken except the law that I was to be back
by four-thirty. The tea made us feel at home together
and Mr. Peebles asked me to call him by his Christian
name, which was Henry; and I laughed when I told
him I already had a name for him—Blinkers, so now
I'd call him Henry Blinkers. He looked rather put out
about being called Blinkers. In the end he laughed,
too; but I realised I'd been unkind and rude, and felt
guilty because all the afternoon I'd been thinking,
'How happy I am! But if only I was with someone
handsome and romantic that I could be proud of, not
just dull old Blinkers who looks like the bark of a tree
and is covered in tweed and leather buttons!' He
wasn't really dull—because he was quite interesting
when he talked—but his face was round and cheerful,
and his blinking eyes were round, too.

While we were having tea, we heard a woodpecker, the first I'd ever heard, and then there was a great squawking noise in the trees and out flew some pinkish birds, larger than pigeons. Blinkers said they were jays and did a lot of damage; but I thought they were beautiful. I saw one walking on a low wall and it was hopping and dancing. I'd been to Wimbledon Common before, but never enjoyed it so much. Blinkers knew all the best and less frequented places. We walked through woods where the leaves were changing colour, and riders galloped past us, and there was a sleepy snake gliding in the sun (it was only called a slow-worm). We came to a small river with high banks decorated with rusty sorrel and willow-herb that had gone like thistledown. Although the water flowed fast, it was faintly brownish, and contained no weeds or fish or any sort of life, and Blinkers said the water was polluted by factories. I noticed the birds were making evening noises, and it suddenly became cold. I remembered home. We hurried back up the cindery horse-ride under the trees. When we came to the windmill, most of the motors and carriages had already gone, and the boy who had been minding our horse looked disconsolate until Blinkers gave him sixpence and the iced cakes we hadn't eaten. I fed the horse with sandwiches with the cucumber taken out.

I didn't enjoy the drive home as much as I had the

drive there because I was so worried in case Father really did something dreadful to me. I could imagine him kicking me until a humped back came or my face was all squashed and ruined. Blinkers became rather worried and wanted to drive me home and come in the house with me, but I knew it would be worse for me afterwards if he did, and I didn't want to be humiliated in front of him.

When we parted at The Trumpet, he told me he would be out of London for the next week or two, but would call on me as soon as he returned. Although he wasn't handsome, I was glad to feel that I was not quite alone.

When I got home, the house was all dark and empty. But as soon as I lit the gas in the hall, the parrot started to laugh and scream, the dogs whined, the cats gave little mews, and the house came to life again. In the kitchen there was a tray of dirty tea-things. I touched the teapot and it was all cold, so I guessed they had been gone a long time and knew I was safe. I felt as if a great weight had been lifted from my chest. I rushed about drawing the curtains, and as I did so, I saw Blinkers on the other side of the street watching the house, and I smiled and waved to him.

Chapter Seven

WHEN I WAS ALONE in the house with Rosa Fisher we
got on quite well, although she made me do all the
work. She would sit on the kitchen table showing her
beautiful hard legs, and watch me as I worked. At
first she talked in her tortured, refined accent; but
soon her great laugh would crack out and crinkles
came at the corners of her rolling eyes. Her talk was
often the kind that is called bawdy, but just as she was
saying something astonishing like, "Oh, I do love a
pair of thick lips," her face would completely change
into a sad clown's and she would wail, "Oh, but I've
had a hard life!" Then she would moan because we
had no front room to sit in and the house was 'given
over to bloody animals'. Already the parrot had been
banished to the downstairs lavatory, and in its boredom
had eaten huge holes in the floor.

When Father was home Rosa hated me and would
shout, "Get out of my way, you snivelling bitch!"
She'd rush round the kitchen cooking the kind of

things Father liked—veal cutlets and mushrooms and food Mother had never thought of. It smelt wonderful, but I was never allowed to eat it. They had their meals in the dining-room and I had to cook myself something and eat it in the kitchen. Every day I became more and more like a maidservant, and I think it slightly worried Father. Once he found me grovelling on the hall floor, polishing, and said, "Get up! Never go on your knees, girl—except to pray!"

I very seldom saw Lucy because we were both working. Lucy was now apprenticed at the Bayswater shop and, although she was free late in the evening, it was just at the time I was washing up the fantastic amount of dishes and utensils Rosa managed to make dirty. Sometimes we met on Sunday afternoon and walked on Clapham Common. Young men would want to walk with us, but they usually had bad teeth and horrid faces under their cloth caps, so we scorned them and walked by ourselves and kicked the fallen leaves. Although we were both seventeen and the same age, Lucy had suddenly gone ahead of me. She talked about the girls in the sewing-room, and, although she couldn't hear or speak to them, she seemed to understand all that went on, and talked about them in a knowing, almost vulgar, way that rather shocked me.

"Our buyer, Miss Burt, thinks she is Lady Muck.

You should see the way she sails into our workroom with her bust all stuck out like a great swan. The lift-man, oh, he's a saucy one! He tries to look up the girl's skirts when they are going upstairs. He hasn't looked up my skirts yet, but then I don't often go upstairs—our workroom is in the basement. A lot of the girls are cripples, the sewing girls. They come in the morning with great crutches, like witches with broomsticks. I'd rather be deaf than lame any day."

I told her about Mr. Peebles, and even said he was almost handsome; but she wasn't at all impressed and said I should get some work away from home as it would broaden my mind. Well, Rosa Fisher was broadening my mind like anything and I didn't enjoy it, but I would have liked to have got away from home. Sometimes the life I was living seemed so hopeless and sad I would try to imagine I was in another world. Then all the dreary brown things in the kitchen would turn into great exotic flowers and I'd be in a kind of jungle, and, when the parrot called from his lavatory prison, he wasn't the parrot, but a great white peacock crying out. I would see enormous leaves almost black against a blazing sky, and the sun shining between them like golden swords; and I could hold out my hands and feel the warmth. The smell of the flowers, a smell rather like peonies, would come to me, and the smell of strange damp earth as well.

Then Rosa would call for more coal, or the gas would want lighting. I'd be back in the kitchen again, and it would be nearly dark and smell like candles when they are blown out.

One day when Father was out, Rosa said, "Come and talk to me, dear," when I was passing the dining-room door, which wasn't closed. I went in and saw she had broken the monkey's skull, with its double set of teeth. It lay in small, dry pieces in the grate, and she saw me looking at them, and laughed. ".Well, can you blame me?" she suddenly shouted. "Who wants a monkey's skull grinning at them day in and day out? I told your father what he could do with it yesterday, and he didn't half like it," and she screamed with laughter. "You know what I mean, don't you, dear? Oh! what a house this is—with parrots in the Gents and monkeys' skulls in the dining-room. And then there's this rug. It's nothing but an old dog's skin." Then in her 'refined' voice: "But, seriously, dear, I want to talk to you. Do you know you've got a gentleman admirer?"

I thought she was going to mention Mr. Peebles, but it was someone quite different.

"The head waiter at the Clarence Hotel—and he's ever so nice, you couldn't help but like him. Do you know, he stood me a double brandy and talked about you all the time. He's seen you with the dogs and thinks you are ever so nice. He likes slim girls, he says, but it is your hair he particularly admires. Goodness, the things he says!" She rolled her eyes and laughed to herself. "Well, aren't you interested?"

I wasn't interested, only afraid. Every day Rosa would talk about my admirer, the head waiter, and every day I grew to hate him more. When I was exercising the dogs, I'd hurry all the time. And then one day he was there. I was sure it was him the moment he appeared from behind a letter-box. He was dressed in a horrible green livery, and his greasy black hair had no hat on it. He didn't even look like a waiter. He looked more like a man who works lifts, and rather as I imagined the liftman that Lucy said looked up girls' skirts. I saw he was grinning at me over the letter-box and then he came towards me. I ran, and as I ran I could hear his laughter. Although I became entangled with the dogs' leads, I escaped, and, when I looked round, he wasn't there. But I thought I could still hear him laughing. After that I made little Hank take the dogs for walks, and although they often pulled him over and he returned with bleeding knees, I was very firm about it. Sometimes I felt heartless when I saw the stunted little figure plodding down the hill, with the dogs pulling in all directions.

The next time Rosa mentioned the head waiter, who had the horrible name of Cuthbert ("But he wants to be known to you as Bertie") I told her I was sure I'd seen him and he was dressed in livery and most repulsive. But she only laughed. "Of course he's a head waiter; he told me so himself, and we had quite a talk about wines and all that kind of thing. He's a real gentleman, and you are a lucky girl. As a matter of fact, I had a bash at him myself, but it was only you he seemed to be interested in. Likes them young, I suppose—but then, you really are a pretty girl. You need dressing up a bit and your hair curling. I must have a go at it with my tongs some time." Then Father came home and she forgot about the disgusting Cuthbert—at least, she never mentioned him in front of Father.

One morning Henry Peebles came to see Father to ask him if he would give a lecture to some veterinary students. He often said Father was the most brilliant vet he had worked with, and I could see that, although he didn't admire Father as a man, he admired his work. I was surprised to see how Father's dark, heavy face lit up at the suggestion, and how animated he became as they discussed the lecture.

I was feeding a litter of red-setter puppies. Each one of the ten puppies had to have its individual saucer to make sure it received the correct amount of milk. It was a long business because they were just learning to lap and often the milk became too cool and had to be warmed again; but I couldn't help loving them as they stood on unsteady legs and licked each other's milky faces. Blinkers and Father examined the puppies and felt their joints to make sure there was no sign of rickets developing; and then Blinkers said to Father he was only staying in London for a few hours and could he take me out to the zoo? I would learn a lot there, he said. Father seemed to agree. He was in such a good mood he would have agreed to anything, and I hurried upstairs to change my clothes. I was so scared Father would suddenly say I couldn't go, but when I came down, he was still talking to Blinkers in the most cheerful way.

Rosa had joined them. I could tell she was furious I was going out. She started grumbling, "What about the shopping? She hasn't done the shopping yet." Father replied, "You will have to do it yourself, for once." When she started swearing in front of Blinkers, Father became sullen again and snarled at me, "Well, if you are going, be quick about it." Rosa went into the surgery and slammed the door, which made the parrot scream. We could still hear it as we hurried down the hill.

I said, "Do you really want to go to the zoo? It's so like home." Blinkers said he'd only suggested it because it would please my father and we could do whatever I liked. I said immediately, "I'd prefer to lunch in a grand restaurant and look at shop-windows."

So that was what we did. I don't think Blinkers liked it very much, but he seemed an unselfish kind of man and put up with it.

It was beautiful across the river, although there were no flowers in window-boxes or tubs and the sunblinds had gone too. We went to Harrods Stores and a man with medals opened the door for us, and we walked on carpets like the moss in the woods my mother had told me about. We went very fast in a lift and I felt as if my insides had somehow got in the wrong place—if there hadn't been other people there it would have been like flying. We looked at glowing materials and wonderful hats, some of enormous width and others very high in the crown with feathers and velvet bows at the side to make them even higher. There were fur coats worth hundreds of pounds, and in another department cloth coats, very narrow at the bottom with wide, low-set sleeves. There was a furniture department, too, and I sat on some of the chairs. I could see why Rosa complained about our dining-room. Blinkers kept wanting to buy me things—long kid gloves, and an embroidery set in a green velvet case with scissors shaped like storks and the blades making the stork's beak—but I didn't like to take these things in case it meant I'd have to marry him one day. In the stationery department there were fountain-pens with special pencils to match, and I couldn't bring myself to refuse one: I'd always wanted a fountain-pen, although I had no one to write to, and thought it almost worth the risk of having to marry Blinkers. They let me try several pens to make sure the nib was the right thickness. I wrote 'Alice, Alice, Alice' in my over-large handwriting and chose the finest nib because I could make wonderful scrolls and flourishes with it. Then Blinkers took a pen and wrote 'Alice Peebles' in large firm writing and we stood there looking at each other until the shop assistant asked impatiently, "Well, have you found a pen that suits you?"

We had lunch in a hotel quite near. It was very grand; but I was a bit disappointed because most of the other people eating there seemed to be quite old—rather fat and middle-aged, really. I'd hoped to see beautiful young people—or rather, wicked ones, the women with enormous hats and black stuff round their eyes, and the men with monocles. The waiters were dark and polite. There was a very large one with a straight back and sticking-out stomach. Blinkers said he was the head waiter. I became terrified of him and couldn't swallow any more—fortunately, the meal was almost over. I kept thinking he was looking at me with his heavy-lidded eyes. When we drank coffee from little gold-edged cups, I told Blinkers about the terrible head waiter admirer Rosa was trying to foist on to me. I could see I'd spoilt his coffee and wished I hadn't mentioned it. His kind face became puckered and distressed. After some minutes' silence, he said, "Rosa is a very dangerous and evil woman, I'm afraid, and I don't like to think of her being in contact with you." His round eyes blinked sadly. "Whatever happens, you mustn't meet this man—this waiter. I wish I wasn't leaving London, but I must go down to Hampshire today. My mother hasn't been at all well, and now, it seems, she has dismissed the companion-housekeeper I'd engaged to look after her. She is living in the house all alone—the worst thing possible for her." He looked at his watch and discovered he was already in danger of missing his train, and I was upset because I'd ruined our lunch. Before we parted, he gave me his mother's address and told me to write to him if I was in any trouble. He added, "Perhaps you would write in any case; you can use your new pen." So I promised I would. It was the least I could do.

Then we parted and I crossed the river and went home. That evening I cut off some of my yellow hair and made a fringe across my forehead. I tried to narrow the bottom of my coat, but it didn't work.

Chapter Eight

IT WAS SUNDAY MORNING, and old people passed me
like sad grey waves on their way to church. The streets
smelt of roasting meat cooked by mothers; and the
pavement was wet, with crushed brown leaves upon
it. A dog stood in the road barking at nothing. When
I came near, it barked at me until a man threw a stone
at it and it ran away howling. It was that kind of day;
but I wasn't really sad because I was returning from
having my new costume fitted—a beautiful grey one,
trimmed with braid, and the skirt was to be so full
behind it was almost a train. It was Rosa who had
persuaded my father that I needed new clothes. Lucy's
mother was making them. I liked to have my fittings
on Sunday because Lucy was there. She would sit on
the music-stool and twist round and round as she
talked on her hands. I couldn't answer much because
I had to keep my hands still while the dressmaker went
round me with pins in her mouth. Lucy admired my
fringe and I admired her hair, which was like a door-

knocker—a doubled-up plait with an enormous black bow on the top. Once when we were going to the front door together, she showed me a book rather like an autograph album. She explained that you rubbed the leaves on your face and powder came off and improved it. Lucy's face was usually a gentle green. Now it was quite white; but I thought I preferred it green.

When I returned home Rosa and Father were drinking port in the dining-room, and the beef that was boiling in the kitchen was nearly dry and the carrots had stuck to the bottom of the saucepan. I added more water, and balls of dough to make dumplings. The dumplings swelled up huge and danced in the boiling gravy, and the kitchen was filled with steam. Water poured down the windows like rain inside out. I began to think I could hear water pouring and falling. Then I thought I could see it, and it was as if floods had come, and everywhere there was water very grey and silvery, and I seemed to be floating above it. I came to a mountain made of very dark water; but, when I reached the top, it was a water garden where everything sparkled. Although the water was rushing very fast, it always stayed in the same beautiful shapes, and there were fountains and trees and flowers all shimmering as if made of moving ice. It was so unbelievably beautiful I felt how privileged I was to see it. Then the birds came, enormous birds slowly flying, and they were made of water, too. Sometimes clouds covered them, but they would appear again, very proud and heavy, and each keeping to his appointed route. This wonderful water world didn't last long because a mist came, and gradually it wasn't there, and something was hurting my head. Somehow I'd managed to fall on the kitchen floor, and knocked my head on a coal scuttle. Coal had got in my hair, but otherwise everything was as it had been before I'd seen the water garden—just boiling beef and steam, and heard Rosa's and Father's voices coming through the wall.

My costume was finished and I collected it, all new and elegant in a box Lucy had smuggled from her shop. I tried it on in my bedroom. I stood on a chair so that I could see the skirt properly in my tiny mirror, and there it was, wide and flowing round my ankles and slightly longer at the back. Then it came into my mind that I'd read somewhere about hobble skirts, and I felt rather saddened. I pulled my skirt tight round my legs, but it didn't look right. Rosa said I hadn't enough calf to my legs, and gentlemen liked a good calf. Then I thought, 'To hell with gentlemen; I've never seen one I liked.'

I climbed down from the chair and ran downstairs to show Rosa how well the costume fitted. She tweaked it and pulled it, and felt the material between her thumb and forefinger, and said I looked "real nice, but I would have preferred a more fancy material myself". Then she said she would take me out to tea the next day to a new place that had just opened in the High Street, where you ate things called pastries and all the customers were ladies and gentlemen. "You'll be surprised, dear, at the people you meet there." Then she suddenly started laughing and rolling her eyes and saying I was 'a scream', although I hadn't said anything at all.

I went away feeling rather silly, and there was my father in the hall. Seeing him unexpectedly like that, I saw him very clearly: he wasn't as large as I'd re-membered him, but quite an ordinary size, and his cheeks hung down rather yellow and sad; only his moustache remained as it had always been—black and fierce and pointed. When he saw me, he jerked his head towards the dining-room and said, "Rosa in there?" and when I said she was, he went in. I could hear angry voices. I guessed Father was angry because Rosa had been out to lunch with another 'gentleman', a "very nice traveller I've known a long time". When she had told me about the traveller, I'd imagined a man in an enormous travelling coat, smelling of trains, and a deerstalker hat, and accompanied by lots of heavy leather trunks; but he wasn't that kind of traveller at all—just a man with a little case filled with hair-oil which he tried to make chemists buy. I stayed in my bedroom till the angry voices ceased. Then I went to keep the parrot company in the downstairs lavatory because he seemed to be pining in there. The house had been quiet for some time when Rosa and Father appeared, all dressed up, and said they were going out for the evening, and I was told all the things I was to do in their absence.

Chapter Nine

ROSA KEPT HER PROMISE and took me out to tea, although the red-setter puppies were howling their heads off and little Hank didn't seem able to manage them very well. I felt rather guilty leaving him all by himself. There was a dying duck, too, that had eaten laburnum seeds and needed a lot of attention, as it seemed to have an unquenchable thirst; so I went into the animals' room to give Hank last instructions. He gazed at me in my new clothes, and said, "Oh, Miss!" and even the puppies stopped howling for a moment. Rosa stood at the door shouting, "Hurry up, do! and leave those blasted animals."

Just as we passed through the rusty iron gate, a small girl with a cat in a bag appeared. The cat's indignant head protruded out of the bag and it was making noises rather like a baby. I stopped to wait for the child, but Rosa pinched my arm, and said, "Come on, for Christ's sake. I've had enough of this," so we passed the child. I looked over my shoulder and saw

73

her standing on the doorstep talking to Hank, and I knew Father would be angry. It might have been an emergency that needed instant attention. Once someone came running to the house with a mad cat in a sack. It had been partly cooked in the oven by mistake. I kept asking Rosa if I could return and telling her about the half-roasted cat, but she impatiently exclaimed, "Fiddlesticks! Don't you ever want to enjoy yourself, you little misery!" And we went on.

We came to the High Street, where shoppers were darting about in all directions followed by children— little girls with their hats low on their brows and their crimped hair flowing and small boys with peaky white faces, eating toffee-apples and scuffling the toes of their boots. I wanted to look in a flower-shop window, but Rosa hustled me on as if we had a train to catch. There was a fascinating hairdresser's window, with wonderful wigs and wax men and women simpering at each other and looking like people from another world; but she wouldn't let me gaze at their bland and innocent faces and fungus-like hair. There was a smell of baking bread, and warm air came up my knickers through gratings in the pavement, and we had arrived at Rosa's tea-shop. In the window stood a wedding-cake that was seven cakes in one, all decorated in white and silver with doves and flowers and little silver shoes; and I thought, 'If only men were like the heroes in books, how lovely it would be to get married and have a cake like that!' Rosa looked at the cake quite longingly, too, and said, "I bet, if I married your father, he'd never buy me a wedding-cake, him being a widower and all," and her face became a sad clown's until we went into the restaurant. Then she began rolling her eyes and smiling.

It wasn't nearly as grand as the hotel dining-room Blinkers had taken me to, but it was nice and clean, and the table-cloth was starched and pure white. Rosa kept saying how smart it was and exclaiming about the silver teapot and the little forks we were given to eat the things called pastries with. She had forgotten her previous impatience and had suddenly become very gay and kept calling me 'dear': "You must forgive me, dear, if I was a little impatient with you earlier on, but we seemed to be wasting all the afternoon and I'd been looking forward to giving you a little treat." I felt rather beastly and ungrateful, and tried to be cheerful. I said how lovely I thought cream horns were, although the pastry got stuck in my throat.

An enormous tabby cat came and sat on the chair next to me and I rubbed its bullet-like old head. Above its faint, hoarse purr, I suddenly heard Rosa say, "Why, Mr. Cuthbert! This is a surprise! Won't you join us for a cup of tea? This is my little friend, Alice." And there was the greasy-haired, cheeky man

75

I'd seen all dressed in green livery, only he was dressed in navy-blue now with stripes. He snatched my hand and shook it up and down, and then suddenly put it to his lips, which caused Rosa to go into shrieks of laughter. Everyone seemed to be looking at us. I pulled my hand away, and could feel my face going red and my eyes filling with tears. The frightful Cuthbert exclaimed, "You are a shy one, and no mistake!"

I endured a few minutes of Cuthbert's conversation, but when I found his hand stroking my thigh, I stood up and told Rosa I was going home. She was angry at first. Then I saw her exchange glances with Cuthbert, and she said, "Well, dear, if you feel like that, we'll all go home together," and we left the tea-shop.

We walked along the High Street together. I was like a prisoner between Rosa and the revolting little man, and hung my head in shame. He pinched my arm and said, "Shy, eh?" I wasn't shy, just ashamed. We turned into another busy street and Rosa said, "I thought we'd just have a little look at the hotel where Mr. Cuthbert works." We came to a large pub painted dark brown. There was an arch which ran through the middle of the building to some stables; and there was fine wire mesh in the windows, with 'Tap Room', 'Dining-room' and 'Lounge' worked in gold. We walked under the arch and I said, "Why are we going here? I want to go home," and Cuthbert said, " 'Arf a mo', dear. I just wanted to show you the talking jackdaw. It's got bright blue eyes and is a real comic little talker." I felt afraid as if I was near something terrible, though there was nothing terrible, just a quiet yard with stables all round and a kind-faced horse was looking out of one, its grey head hanging over the door. My throat felt all dry and tight and I couldn't speak. Rosa gripped my arm very hard and Cuthbert held the other.

We came to the jackdaw's cage. There he was hopping about just like any other bird except that his eyes were blue and he didn't say a word. We were right at the end of the yard now. Through an open door I could see a saddle-room with a little fire burning in the grate. We stood in front of the bird's cage and nobody said anything, but Cuthbert gave Rosa a cigarette and when he went to light it he struck the match across his teeth only using one hand. Then Rosa suddenly let go of my arm. I nearly fell because my legs felt so weak. I hardly knew how it had happened, but Cuthbert had dragged me into the saddle-room and we were there together. Rosa had gone. I tried to open the door, but it wouldn't open. Cuthbert laughed and said, "Come on, now, don't be coy," and then his dreadful face was close to mine and he was kissing me and tearing at my clothes. He dragged me down to the floor, and we were linked together. I tried to scream, but no noise came. Then I started to bite, and bit his face and bit it till I could taste salt blood in my mouth. He gave me a great blow on the head, but still I bit, and then I was free and he wasn't touching me at all, and suddenly I found I could scream. When he put his hand over my mouth, I bit again. Then he stood up and started kicking me as I lay on the ground, but I could still scream. He muttered, "Shut up, you bloody little fool!' Then he opened the door and ran away.

I lay on the floor, too frightened to move, but he didn't come back. Somehow I managed to stagger to my feet. My head was throbbing and wouldn't come straight, but hung down on one shoulder. In the darkness bright lights seemed to appear in my eyes, like giant sparkler fireworks. I didn't notice all the pains that had come until I walked, and then they were all over me. I felt very tired and dirty. In the darkness I tried to find my gloves—my belt had gone as well as part of my blouse, and, as I stumbled about, I found I was repeating my twelve times table, although I'd never known it properly before. I remembered the lessons I'd learnt in the little school I'd attended with Lucy. There was a laurel hedge very near the window, and the revolving globe of the world was really a tin biscuit-barrel. For a minute I could even smell exercise-books and ink, and remember the fascination of mastering the figure eight so that it wasn't a little circle on a slightly larger circle but a beautiful twisting shape.

I touched my cheeks. They were stiff with Cuthbert's dirty dried blood, and my lips were swollen, too. I felt my teeth because they hurt and I thought they might be all broken; but they were still there, smooth and firm in my mouth. I thought, 'There is no hope for me—no hope at all,' and slow tears mixed with the dirty blood on my face. I dragged myself out of that frightful little room and somehow reached the street. The lamps were lit, all shining on me in my disgrace, and I saw people looking at me, so I turned my face to the wall and pushed my hair over it. The big black hat I'd been wearing wasn't there any more and I was glad it belonged to Rosa and was probably all torn and crushed now.

I stood outside our house. I could see my father in the gaslight standing by his roll-top desk sort of snarling to himself. I dared not go into the house all pulled about and stained; so I stood there in the road until I saw Rosa come into Father's room, smiling her forced, bright smile. She came towards the window. Perhaps she only meant to pull the curtains; but I was afraid of her, and ran away where it was dark. I kept to the dark little streets until I found myself in the street where Mrs. Churchill lived. I remembered she had said she would be my friend, and I went to her house. There was music coming out and I knew it must be 'our Vera' playing the piano; but it stopped when I knocked at the door, and the bark of dogs came instead. In the dark little hall Mrs. Churchill came and let me into her house. She took me to her front room, where her daughter Vera sat at the piano in her pink blouse. Vera screamed when she saw me and Mrs. Churchill cried, "Oh Lors!" and suddenly I felt damp round my mouth and a sort of singing came, and I was falling.

They said I'd fainted. I lay on a red plush couch, and felt the pile with my finger-nails. Mrs. Churchill was bathing my face and mopping at it with a towel that smelt sour, and Vera was standing by with a cup of tea. In front of the fire the two fattest dogs I d ever seen lay panting and scratching. I drank the tea to please them, although it was difficult because when I sat up my head hurt so much. The room was very hot and bright and they were so kind; even the panting dogs before the fire had kind faces. I told them about Rosa and the terrible Cuthbert and the jackdaw with blue eyes; but I couldn't tell them everything because I was so ashamed—however many baths I had I'd never be really clean again. They lent me an enormous night-dress of Mrs. Churchill's and let me sleep on the sofa under dark blankets. I lay there, very hot, and listened to their voices the other side of the wall. Once I heard a child cry out and thought it must be Vera's boy; once I heard the deep voice of 'Dad', who sounded as if he was talking through a greasy bowler hat.

In the night I was awake and floating. As I went up, the blankets fell to the floor. I could feel nothing below me—and nothing above until I came near the ceiling and it was hard to breathe there. I thought, 'I mustn't break the gas globe.' I felt it carefully with my hands, and something very light fell in them, and it was the broken mantle. I kept very still up there because I was afraid of breaking other things in that small crowded room; but quite soon, it seemed, I was gently coming down again. I folded my hands over my chest and kept very straight, and floated down to the couch where I'd been lying. I was not afraid, but very calm and peaceful. In the morning I knew it wasn't a dream because the blankets were still on the floor and I saw the gas mantle was broken and the chalky powder was still on my hands.

Chapter Ten

I WENT BACK to my father's house the next day, but Mrs. Churchill had been before me: Rosa had gone. Father opened the door. He turned away from my bruised face and went back to the animals' room. There was no Rosa sitting huddled over the dining-room fire, complaining and laughing and complaining again. I went up to her room. It was still all pink, but the bed was unmade and she wasn't there. I opened the cupboard almost expecting her to jump out at me; but it was empty except for some dirty ribbon and moth balls. She had really gone, although I could still smell her scent. I opened the window and let the dark afternoon in, and, as I did so, I heard the front door slam. I knew Father had gone out and I was alone.

The days went on. I tried to look after Father well, so that Rosa didn't come back. Mrs. Churchill came every morning, and we sat in the kitchen drinking tea again; but now she didn't talk about her garden: it was

Christmas all the time. "You must see the novelties I've collected, you really should, and the little dolls I've dressed for the girls. Vera's boy is to have a humming-top and my other grandson, handcuffs. Just toy ones, of course, but he may as well get used to them; you never know what may happen in life, do you?"

It seemed she always had about fifty people to her little house at Christmas, and they all had something to eat and drink and a present. I thought of our sad Christmas, when never a friend came to the house, or even a card through the letter-box; only enormous calendars, advertising cattle food and animals' medicines.

I wrote a letter to Blinkers. Although it wasn't very long, it took me two weeks to write because it was the first one I'd ever written—there had been no one to write to before. I told him that the weather was nice for the time of year, and that all the red-setter puppies had gone, and that Rosa had gone as well. I told him something terrible nearly happened to me in a saddle-room, but Mrs. Churchill said I was still a good girl, and although I had nasty dreams at night, I did not have them so often as I did at first. I told him that I was quite well and always his friend. It wasn't a long letter, but it did take so long to write; and afterwards I was worried in case I should have left out the part

83

about the saddle-room, and I thought, 'He'll never want me to be Alice Peebles now.'

Every morning I did the shopping, and, although there were so many people in the streets, I was always afraid of seeing Cuthbert. Sometimes I thought I did, and I'd run into a shop feeling dreadfully sick and shaky; but when I looked through the door he wouldn't be there at all. I expect I imagined him. Mrs. Churchill said Father had complained to the hotel where he worked and he'd been sent away, but I worried in case he hadn't been sent away far enough.

It was almost dark when I went to post Blinkers's letter. I remembered how I'd once seen Cuthbert all green behind the scarlet pillar-box, so I went to one farther away. I took a little white dog with me for protection. He had been sent to Father because his ears stuck up like little sails instead of neatly folding down beside his eyes. Now his ears had lumps of lead fixed to them with cobbler's wax and hung sadly down, and the poor dog kept shaking his head and trying to get the lead off with his paws.

In the dusk I suddenly came close to someone. I smelt Rosa's scent, and in the greyness she was there. She touched me. I could see her face quite clearly and thought, 'She is like a white negress.' Then she put her sad clown's face on and spoke with her refined voice with the twisted vowels, "Well, dear, I've been wondering if I'd see you. It's quite a time since we last met, and I want to have a little talk."

"No, no, I don't want to talk," I cried as I tried to free myself from her gripping fingers. But I knew I'd never get away. The little dog seemed to know it, too, and it sat at my feet shaking its weighted ears.

"Christ! what's wrong with that dog's ears?" Rosa muttered. Then she recollected herself. "I know you must feel a little annoyed with me, dear. But how was I to know Mr. Cuthbert was only a porter? I wouldn't have encouraged him if I'd known, but he told me he was a head waiter, and I must say he knew all about wines. Real deceitful, he was, to us both. He was a married man, too, with a wife and kids in Birmingham, but he told me he was single and I thought he was just the chap for you—liven you up a bit!" She turned her head from side to side and her eyes became all crinkly at the corners. "Oh, but he was a scream! D'y'know, he could strike matches on his teeth!"

I turned away, but she gripped my arm again. "Don't go, Alice, I'm really sorry about what happened. I meant well, and now Mr. Cuthbert has been sent away, can't we be friends? Tell your father you met me and say we are friends again. Tell him I miss him, and Alice . . ."

She suddenly began to cough, and her whole body

was shaken by great husky coughs. Her grip on my arms relaxed and I was able to free myself. For a moment I stood still. Then I ran and left her there still in the dusk, still coughing. I felt ashamed of leaving her like that, all doubled up and helpless, but I had to escape. When I arrived home, the parrot's cries greeted me from the hall. I remembered how Rosa had banished him to the lavatory and how depressed he'd been in there, pecking away at the floor-boards until large holes had come. I drew the dining-room curtains and stirred up the fire and looked at the empty leather chair where Rosa used to sit and complain, and I was glad it was empty and that she was out in the dark, coughing by herself.

I did not tell Father I'd met Rosa. In any case, we rarely spoke to each other—just now and then about the animals and meals. Often, when we ate our lunch together, we never spoke a word, and, when I went into the kitchen to fetch the pudding, I'd start talking to myself because I felt so stiff and nervous. I'd even talk to the pudding, "Come on, Old Apple Pie, you've got to be eaten now. I hope you taste better than you look. Now, Plate, I can't possibly use you. Don't you know you have a great chip on your side? Here's a better one, but, now I see you properly, I find there is dried mustard on you—how provoking you are! Here you are, Tray, you have got to do some work for once." Then I would return to the dining-room, and there would be my father leaning back in his chair, biting his moustache and drumming his square fingers on the table. He always tucked a napkin in his collar, and against its whiteness his face was very sallow. It seemed to have grown smaller lately. In fact, he seemed to have shrunk all over, and I hoped it wasn't my cooking that had made this happen.

I told Mrs. Churchill I'd seen Rosa, and she said, "Oh, the perisher! Trying to come back, is she?" She scrubbed the kitchen floor angrily, her square old face red and fierce. She knelt there in the dirty water, with her legs sticking out behind and pink bloomers show-ing below her knees, and muttered, half to herself, "They won't take her back at The Trumpet and I don't blame them: people know too much about her round here. She'll have to get a job the other side of the river—and good riddance!" Then she unexpectedly smiled as she plunged her brush in the bucket before smearing soap on it. "Do you know, they have Snow White and the Seven Dwarfs all made of soap in the window of a chemist in Lavender Hill. Really lovely thing it is. Just imagine rubbing a dwarf's beard on your flannel!" So Rosa was forgotten and it was Christmas novelties again.

That evening Lucy came to see me. While Rosa had been there, her mother wouldn't allow her to visit the house, but now she came and we sat in the kitchen, looking at fashion-books that were no longer fashionable, and talking to each other with our hands. I heard the front-door bell ring, but Father answered it. Someone went into his surgery, and the heavy door closed.

Chapter Eleven

IT WAS AFTER BREAKFAST, and I went into the dining-room to clear away the remains of Father's kippers. The sun came slanting in through the window and touched the mantelpiece, where the monkey's skull used to lie. I placed a damp log on the recently lighted fire. A soft hissing sound came and a frantic wood-louse rushed about the smoking bark. I rescued it with a teaspoon, although I had no fondness for woodlice. It was a pity to let it burn—and there it was, squirming on the damp tea-spoon, grey and rather horrible. With one hand I pushed up the window and with the other placed it on the sill, where it crawled about leaving a small wet trail of tea among the winged sycamore-seeds that had lodged there. The air was sharp and wintry, and the street very still. The only people to be seen were a few pale women with black string bags. Under the gate a dried leaf rustled very gently. I thought, 'It's minutes like this that seem to last so long.'

The door-handle rattled and Father came into the room behind me. I hurried to the table and started collecting the breakfast remains. He stood over me, glowering. "If you want the window open, why the hell don't you let the fire out?" I ran to close the window, and, while my back was turned, he almost shouted, "You're leaving here—going to stay with Peebles's mother. It was arranged last night. He may come round and talk to you about it some time to-day."

I'd turned round and was staring at him in bewilderment. "I'm off!" he bellowed at me, and slammed the door. A few minutes later I saw him leave the house with his case in his hand and his bowler hat pushed far back on his head. The iron gate clanked and he'd gone; but, even if he'd remained, I wouldn't have dared to ask why I was being sent away like this.

The morning went on and Henry Peebles didn't come. I began to think that perhaps it wasn't true, that I wasn't going away at all. At first I'd been afraid of leaving home and going to a strange woman's house, but now I began to realise that nothing could be worse than home. If Mrs. Peebles was like her son, at least she would be kind. I wondered where Mrs. Peebles lived, and then I remembered the address Blinkers had given me: it was Hampshire and an island. It would have been wonderful if it had been

Wales and I could have seen the farm where my mother used to live. In my mind I had a picture of my mother's part of Wales. It was always the spring and very, very green, with the sun sparkling on waterfalls and wet slate roofs; there were impossibly high mountains, and wild goats, with enormous horns, were dotted about. I tried to imagine Mrs. Peebles's island; but I could only think of desert islands with palm trees, and Blinkers didn't look as if he came from anywhere like that.

In the afternoon I made a currant cake, but my mind was on other things, and the currants all went to the bottom and the cake stuck in the tin and broke as I was getting it out. As I stood looking down at this wreck of a cake, Henry Peebles arrived. I let him in and he said, "What a heavenly smell—just like Christmas cake!" and went straight to the kitchen. Even while I'd been to the front door, worse things had happened to the wretched cake, and now it had fallen in half.

"What on earth can I do with a cake like that?" I asked, bitterly.

Blinkers replied, "There is only one thing to do with it: eat it while it's hot."

So I made some tea and we ate broken cake with it. All the time I was waiting for him to say something about this visit to his mother's, but he didn't for ages, not until we'd almost eaten the whole cake and I'd begun to wish I hadn't. Then he said I was to be a companion to his mother. She had some people living on the ground floor of her house, but, although they did the work, they were no company for her. She was a little strange in her ways, it seemed, very remote and sometimes depressed; but I was to be an interest for her, and we were to look after each other, and it was going to be a great success. Blinkers beamed on me with his kind, blinking eyes, and I said I hoped his mother would like me. "Of course she will," he exclaimed. "She'll love you." And he gently stroked my bare arm and I knew he still wanted me to be Alice Peebles.

Then Father came home and there was nothing for his tea except the remains of broken cake, cold and heavy now.

It was all arranged and I was to leave home in less than a week. Father became almost pleasant to me now I was going: it was such a relief to his mind. I think that I must have reminded him of Mother, and also that he couldn't bear feeling that he was responsible for one he disliked and despised. Often I'd thought I must be despicable and low or he wouldn't feel like this about me. At other times some of his fierceness seemed to rise in me and I'd long to shout at him, "It's you that are despicable! I'd be all right if I were away from here. Blast and damn you!" But, of course, I never dared. I should think it's a dreadful sin to swear at your father, though no worse than for a father to swear at his daughter. Anyway, now he didn't swear at me, or turn away when he had to speak to me. He was abrupt and impatient, but quite thoughtful and reasonable, and he sometimes spoke to me at meal-times. Once, when we were eating liver, he suddenly said, "You'll find it cold in the country and there will be warm clothes to be bought—a coat . . . a dress . . . I don't know, but get Mrs. Churchill to go through your things and make a list. No black, mind. I won't pay for mourning clothes."

Mrs. Churchill was delighted I was going. In a way it rather annoyed me—everyone glad I was going— but I knew Mrs. Churchill thought it was for my own good. She kept saying, "It's all that nice Mr. Peebles's doing. I could kiss him, that I could. He's really nice, considering he's a man." The thought of Blinkers's surprise if suddenly embraced by Mrs. Churchill made me laugh and wish she would carry out her threat. Every time he came to the front door, she beamed on him and kept giving him little pats as he walked down the hall. Even Father seemed to like him. I did, too: but sometimes he made me feel suffocated, perhaps because I wasn't used to kindness. There would be his

93

gentle eyes looking at me in a swamping way, and I'd keep thinking, 'I must be grateful'; there we would be sitting on the stiff dining-room chairs, Blinkers being kind and me grateful.

He told me he was buying a partnership with a vet the other side of the river, in a place called Earl's Court. There weren't any earls there, but there were many old ladies with small dogs and large cats that needed constant attention. He said he was going to grow very rich and retire to the country, and in the meantime, he would take off his hat to every Pekinese he met.

Father gave money to Mrs. Churchill to buy me new clothes, but she refused to "cross the water" and we had to shop in Brixton. All the same, I did manage to get a wonderful coat, dark green with braid, and cut on rather military lines. It had a sort of pill-box hat to match, and cost so much we had only enough money left for a green skirt and two flannel morning blouses and a real silk one for afternoons. There was no money for underclothes at all, so I'd just have to manage with the old things I already possessed. "We mustn't let old Moustaches know you're going all ragged underneath or he'll make us return that fine coat. Silly old fool! A nice coat's more important to a girl than woollen knickers, any day."

Mrs. Peebles didn't write to me. I would have liked a welcoming letter, but her son said she was expecting

me and the room he had had as a boy had been prepared for me—"although I'd have liked it better if
she'd given you one looking over the creek," he added.
I wasn't sure what a creek was, so I didn't particularly
care if I saw one from my window or not. I cared
much more that Mrs. Peebles should like me.

My last day at home the vivisectionist's man came,
with his pointed, yellow shoes, and it rained from
heavy, grey, mushroomy clouds. On a bench in the
hall damp people with damp animals sat waiting to see
Father. The parrot shivered on his perch. He had
never been the same since he had lived in the lavatory,
and now he had started pulling out his own feathers
and bald patches had come, revealing pale and scaly
skin.

My clothes were packed in a black trunk that had
belonged to my mother. Each time I went into my
bedroom, there it was, with labels tied on the handles,
and I'd sit on my bed looking at it, wondering what
kind of a home we'd be in tomorrow, my trunk and
I. Downstairs Mrs. Churchill mopped muddy foot-
marks from the hall for the third time, and her bulldog face looked closed and cross under her cloth cap;
then she put on her macintosh, which was greasy round
the neck, and departed.

It was little Hank's turn to leave next. He came
clumping out of the animals' room, his heavy face

white and tired. I suddenly felt sorry for the exhausted child, so poor and underfed, and called him into the kitchen. He came in slowly, dragging his feet, half expecting to be scolded for some work left undone, and I cut a large slice of fruit cake and handed it to him, expecting him to grab it. He took it very slowly and looked at it intently. Surprised, I asked him why he didn't eat it, and he mumbled, " 'Cos I want to remember what it looked like when it'd gone." Then he stood by the kitchen door eating his cake with very small bites. When it was finished, he picked up a few fallen currants from the floor and ate them one by one, then crept from the room without saying a word and left the house.

When I went to clear away Father's tea, he was sitting with his square hands on the table, either side of his plate, all smeared now with congealed food. I put the dirty china on a tray. I hardly liked to touch the plate between his dreadful hands; even his fingers had black hairs on them. To my relief, he abruptly left the table and sat in the leather chair. I could feel he was looking at me and my hands shook as I tried to clear away. He suddenly shouted, "Hurry up, girl; for Christ's sake, stop dithering! I want to speak to you." Somehow I managed to take the things into the kitchen, but when I returned, in my nervousness I knocked the door and started the dogs across the hall barking. I went into the room, and there was Father still looking at me. I stood by the door holding the handle so that I could escape quickly if necessary. He took a cachou from the silver box on his watch-chain and, as he crunched it, he still went on looking at me, and the sweet smell, which I connected with my father, made me even more afraid, although to other people it must seem quite harmless. Suddenly he began to talk, and it was as if he'd rehearsed it.

"There are things that should be said between us and I'm saying them now. The main thing is that you're leaving this house tomorrow. I hope I shall never see you again. This young man Peebles seems to have taken to you—and, by God! he can keep you. You've never been a child of mine. Did you know you couldn't walk until you were two? It used to make me sick to see you clapping about on your bottom instead of walking like a decent child. Look at you now, sickly and pale, like a washed-out clout, and no flesh on you at all. But, although you're a miserable thing and no child of mine, have I ever stinted you? Tell me that!"

"No, Father," I whispered.

He gave me a withering glance, and went on, "Did you know I married your mother for a miserable hundred pounds? If I'd waited a year, even less than a year, I'd have had ten times that amount of money, but

97

your mother trapped me with her miserable hundred. I might have forgiven her if she had produced a son, but she wasn't even capable of that. Her brothers used to call her 'the singing mouse', among other silly pet-names; but I soon made her sing out of the wrong side of her mouth, and she deserved it. But I never stinted her."

His voice fell and his eyes weren't looking at me any more. He was talking to someone else. "I never stinted you, although you were less to me than a house-keeper. I could have turned you out for your deceit and sickly ways, but I let you stay here as Mrs. Rowlands, although I loathed the sight of you and your finicky daughter. Now you are dead, and it's better for us both. You were rotting away with a filthy disease; you are better dead, I tell you. I never stinted you; it was you that stinted yourself. I gave you a fine coffin. What more do you want? Is it your paper-white daughter . . ."

My father did not notice when I left the room.

Chapter Twelve

IT WAS THE MORNING when I was to leave home. Sad November sun shone through the stained glass in the hall and made horrible patterns on Father as he stood at the foot of the stairs, waiting for me to go. Henry Peebles arrived in a cab to take me and my black trunk to the station, and Father gave him the money for a single ticket that was going to take me away. The cab-driver put my trunk upon his shoulder and went out of the door, bending under the weight. It was time to leave.

I said, "Good-bye, Father," and he said, "Good-bye, Alice." It was the first time I'd ever heard him call me by my name. As I followed the cabman through the door, I turned and looked at Father. He still stood there in the hall, with the worn Turkey carpet beneath him, and, now the door was open, it was clear sun that shone upon him. So I left the house, and Blinkers put me on the train.

For a long time it was London that flashed past the

windows; then the green, but leafless, country came, and fields with cows and sheep. I never knew there were so many kinds of cows before, all different colours; some even had no horns at all, and I saw a bull wearing a dreadful mask over his face. Watching these things and worrying about my trunk, which a porter had taken right away, kept me occupied at first. Then I began to study my fellow passengers.

Blinkers had put me in a second-class ladies' carriage, although I would have preferred a first-class smoking one. In the corner seat opposite me was a scraggy woman with a fringe, dressed in lolly pink. She told me before the journey was over that she resembled Queen Alexandra. I was surprised. She made me change seats with her because, she said, she was always sick if her back faced the engine. I didn't want her to be sick, so I changed, and the view from the window was all going the wrong way. A grey-haired, monumental woman with a drooping mouth began to ask me questions about my family and where I was going. As she moved she creaked, she was so clamped into her corsets. She was a town councillor's wife from Wimbledon, and she ignored the lolly pink woman. There was another occupant of the carriage. She was a small spinster lady who kept smiling to herself. She was making face-flannels from old towels, putting coloured crochet round the edges. She said they were intended for Christmas presents, and I thought I'd write and tell Mrs. Churchill about them because they might be what she called 'novelties'—only I couldn't imagine anything Mrs. Churchill had made looking very clean.

I had a little parcel with me of sandwiches she had prepared for me that morning, but I felt too shy to eat them in the train in front of these strange women. At two o'clock I still had not dared to eat my sandwiches and it was the end of the journey—at least, the train part. I began to feel sick and wondered if it was a mistake to sit with my back to the engine. I put the parcel of sandwiches under my seat, but the councillor's wife saw them and said I wasn't to waste good food, I'd be glad of them later, so I had to grovel on the floor and pick them up.

When I got out of the train, I was filled with apprehension about my trunk, and stood on the platform helplessly biting the fingers of my gloves while I watched the train steam out. Most likely it had taken everything I owned and all I would have would be a used railway-ticket and the clothes I was wearing. When the train had gone and it was quiet, I heard pigeons cooing to themselves and saw near me, on a trolly, baskets all filled with birds. Some had labels, asking people to let them loose at certain times. I could imagine the birds' grateful surprise when the lid of the basket was suddenly opened: their little shining eyes would flick for a moment and the cooing would stop; then suddenly they would fly together in a cloud with the sun upon them.

Thinking about the pigeons calmed me a little, and I broke my sandwiches and pushed the crumbs through the baskets and ate some of the ham myself. I looked round the station and saw a group of people and a porter milling round a pile of luggage. Among the luggage was my trunk, larger than anyone else's. I made my way towards it, rather rudely pushing other people, and, grasping one of the handles, said, "That's mine," but no one listened. All the luggage except mine soon disappeared, and, when the porter asked me if I wanted any help, I shook my head because I didn't know what was meant to happen next. Then a man called Povey-the-Carrier came and asked if I was Alice Rowlands. It was lovely to hear my own name, although the voice was different to the ones I was used to.

Povey-the-Carrier drove me away from the station. Soon we came to the water, but the tide was out and it wasn't the sea, only a sort of river, which we crossed over a toll bridge. There were a few boats lying on their sides in the mud in the golden afternoon sun. The very flatness of the Island was beautiful, although I'd been expecting mountains. The air was very fresh, yet soft against my face, and suddenly I was filled with hope and not at all anxious. I thought how happy my mother's ghost must be feeling at my good fortune. Long, rustling grass moved in the afternoon wind and bare trees lined the narrow roads. I'd never really seen the country before. Although I'd enjoyed the view from the train windows, it wasn't the same to see it flashing past, all remote through glass, like a painting. Now I was really in the scenery, and I could hear it, too: the cries of strange sea birds and the sinister caw of rooks as we passed under a whole village of great untidy nests. We passed a farm where there were huge white birds with little heads, and they made a kind of singing sound as we passed. A woman stood by an open gate calling to her cows, and they all came to her in a stately procession without anyone driving them. A pheasant uttered a startled cry and fluttered from a hedge as we approached, and one long feather fell from its tail and floated gently down. I asked Povey-the-Carrier questions about nearly everything we saw. He answered me very slowly, as if he had been speaking to a foreigner or a very young child, starting with such remarks as, "Have you no pheasants in London, now?" or "Don't your dad keep a goose, now? They make fine watchdogs." But I think I really shocked him when I asked how long it would be before his pony grew into a horse.

We drove through narrow lanes that twisted and turned like snakes. Then we came near a farm with a large pond in front of it, and turned down a road that looked too narrow to lead anywhere, but in fact led straight to Mrs. Peebles's house. Suddenly the house appeared, much larger than I expected. It was dark because it was all dressed in ivy and in front of it stood strange light green trees shaped like peg-tops. An ugly and heavy brown porch had been built round the front door, which gave it a gloomy aspect, and the whole place had an unoccupied appearance.

As I was climbing down from the cart, the door of the porch suddenly opened and a tubby little woman, wearing an enormous, dirty, white apron, appeared. She was holding an almost hairless broom, and, when she saw I'd arrived, she put her black-booted feet either side of the broom and started jumping up and down on it in her excitement. I thought, 'Good heavens! this can't be Blinkers's mother,' and in horror I walked towards her. She was still jumping about like a little goblin. She peered at me through her steel-rimmed spectacles as she exclaimed, "I'm Mrs. Gowley—a fellow Londoner. My husband and me run this 'ouse, if yer can call it a 'ouse"—and she went into peals of spiteful laughter. I looked at Povey-the-Carrier and he gave me a reassuring wink, so I thought, 'It's all right, she's only a bit dotty,' and ignored her. She peered at my trunk as he carried it in; then she peered at me as I walked up the steps, and said, "There's not much fat on you, and your face is real peaky. You and Mrs. Peebles will make a fine pair."

I passed through the porch and into the long, stone-flagged hall. The first thing I noticed was the strange light: there appeared to be no window, but daylight came filtering down from the ceiling. When I looked up, I saw the whole ceiling was an elaborate iron grating and the light was coming from a skylight above. The staircase was made of ironwork, too. I followed the awful Gowley goblin up these clanking stairs. I had to walk with great care or the heels of my shoes would have become entangled in the ironwork, but the Gowley clumped ahead of me in her big boots. When we reached the landing, I looked through the grating into the hall and felt an odd insecure feeling at seeing the light coming up like that.

We clanked along the corridor until we faced a short flight of wide stairs—stairs with real carpet on them—and came to three white doors that opened on to a little landing. This landing was solid and covered in linoleum, and there were small furry mats outside each door. The Gowley went to one of the doors and, after unashamedly peering through the keyhole, knocked loudly. I heard no answer, but she flung the door open and marched inside. " 'Ere's the young lady, Mrs. Peebles; 'ere she is!" Uninvited, she sat down in a chair and said, "Mr. Gowley and me are going out this evening, so you'll have to do the boiler yourself—or it can go out for all we care. I can't think what you want with all that hot water."

An immensely tall, thin woman got up from a sofa by the window. She looked at the dreadful Gowley disdainfully, and ordered her to leave the room. For a minute the squat little woman sat with her legs apart in her chair, a spiteful grin across her face; then she got to her feet, shaking her head in a pretended bewildered way, and said, "Oh well, I only hope you two get on. And don't forget, mind: I've told yer about the boiler." She chuckled to herself as she left the room. I heard her stop on the landing outside the door, and thought I could see the awful glint of her spectacles at the key-hole.

Still looking at the door, I said, "She hasn't gone. Do you know she looks and listens at the keyhole?" I turned towards Mrs. Peebles, and there she was, all humped up on the sofa, softly crying to herself. It was terrible to see her like that—so very long, long and sad, she seemed. I walked towards her to put my hand on her poor thin shoulder; but she shook me off and cried, "Don't touch me! Leave me alone!" I stood there staring, too afraid to move; even if I'd run away, there would be the dreadful Mrs. Gowley to pass and the iron staircase and landing.

Then with an effort she began to straighten and looked at me with her great brimming eyes and in a quavering voice, said, "Why, you are only a child. Come and sit by me, dear, and forgive me for my foolish behaviour. It's that dreadful woman. Ever since I had my trouble there has been some repulsive creature living here, but she is the worst—it's the peering and the rudeness. But you haven't seen the husband. He is absolutely sinister, and he squints, my dear, and I'm sure he drinks. My son engaged them in a hurry because he won't let me be alone here—and the doctor's the same." She turned away from me. "Oh! how I long to be alone!"

I stood looking at her, wondering if I should leave the room, but she suddenly gave me an unexpectedly sweet smile and asked me to sit beside her.

So we sat together in the darkening room and became friends. She told me that Henry said I was in danger at home, and I thought he must have been referring to the dreadful Cuthbert. I hoped he hadn't mentioned anything about it to his mother, but if he had, she didn't say so. She seemed to be obsessed with the Gowleys and the hope that I would protect her from them.

It became almost dark in the big room except for the

glow from the fire, and I longed to draw the curtains and make it light; I thought I could see a tall brass lamp gleaming, and on the mantelpiece there were candles waiting to be lit. The vague, sad voice went on and on:

"My husband was still alive when the house was almost gutted by fire. I'll never forget old Floss howling. But we couldn't reach her: there we were trapped in this very room, and smoke pouring under the door. Henry was safe in the next room, but poor old Floss died—and the little maid we had then (I believe her name was Alice too); her charred body was found crouching on the landing. I thought she'd be black like burnt paper—she was a dreadful reddish-brown. Poor girl! I sometimes think the fire was the cause of my trouble."

On and on she went. I'd have been interested if I hadn't been so hungry and tired. At last I dared to interrupt her in the midst of a long story about a pet bear that was only fed on loaves of bread and how it escaped and went to church. I think it was the mention of bread that gave me courage. I asked if she would like me to make some tea. She answered, "Not particularly," and went on about the bear for a little: then suddenly said, "Would you?"

Bewildered, I answered, "Would I what?"

"Would you like some tea?"

"Well, I would rather."

"Oh, dear! Have I been rude? I should have offered you tea as soon as you arrived and now it is dark. We will never be able to make tea in the dark." She got up from the sofa and started fussing about the mantelpiece for matches. I noticed some coloured spills in a vase and lit one from the fire, and soon the candles were giving their flickering, gentle light. I wanted more and more light. I lit the lamp, and waited impatiently while the glass funnel warmed before I could turn it to its full strength. Mrs. Peebles was ineffectually tugging at the grey velvet curtains. I drew the curtains for her and made up the fire and stirred it to a blaze. Looking round the room I was surprised to see how elegant this upstairs drawing-room was; the pale blue carpet, decorated with roses and true lovers' knots, pleased me so much that I almost forgot my hunger. There was a glass-fronted cabinet filled with delicate china; and pretty little chairs and sofas with curved legs were dotted round the room. There were lovely glass things like heavy tinkerbells on the mantelpiece. It was the largest and most enchanting room I'd ever seen.

Mrs. Peebles carried a little lamp and we went clanking along the iron landing past brown-grained doors. I wondered exactly where the other Alice's burnt body had been found. At the end of the landing we came to a room which had been converted into an upstairs kitchen. There were two doors to this kitchen, and later I learnt the other led to two terrible rooms that were completely black and burnt. The remains of charred furniture still stood in them forlornly against the blackened walls. There was a twisted frame of an iron bedstead like some tortured skeleton, and at the glass-less windows the ragged remains of brittle black curtains crumbled.

In Mrs. Peebles's kitchen you could hear grumbling voices from below. Although the floor had lino on it, the lino now had holes, and light as well as voices came through. If you looked through the iron holes, there would be the Gowleys and their dirty kitchen and sour smell. Mrs. Peebles boiled a kettle on a small spirit stove and made pale tea in a silver teapot; and we drank it out of flowered and fragile cups in a medium-sized dining-room with massive furniture.

Chapter Thirteen

I LAY THAT NIGHT for the first time in my little room over the hall. The bed was most comfortable, and I was just drifting off to sleep when a strange thing happened: I seemed to be floating. I tried to touch the mattress with my hands; but it wasn't there. I was floating above it and the bedclothes were slipping from me. In the darkness I was moving up and up— although my stomach felt as if it had been left behind and I think I must have almost touched the ceiling. I did not try to feel it with my hands, because I kept them—I can't think why—neatly folded on my chest. I suddenly realised I was feeling sick. I thought, 'This is bed-sickness, not sea-sickness.' This seemed to me rather witty and I began to laugh, which caused me to descend quickly, and I found myself on the bed again —only my legs were hanging over the end. I lay there for a few minutes, weird thoughts running through my mind. Then I realised how cold I was and got up and re-made the bed. I tucked the clothes in very tight and crept inside, and this time I stayed there, as far as I know, for I slept until morning noises disturbed me.

It was almost light when I awoke, and I judged it to be about eight o'clock. I lay there, warm and sleepy, thinking about the strange occurrence of the night. I remembered how a similar thing had happened to me in Mrs. Churchill's queer little front room; and I thought to myself that anyone but me would under-stand what caused them to float away from their bed in this puzzling way. Perhaps Rosa was right and I was a bit simple. I suddenly felt lonely and depressed. Downstairs I could hear the Gowleys snarling to each other.

I got out of bed and explored my room, which I'd only seen by candle-light the previous evening. It was about the same size as my room at home, and the walls were colour-washed a buttercup yellow, which I thought rather attractive. There was a bookshelf running right across one wall, but the books were dis-appointing, all schoolboy stuff: I looked in vain for Mrs. Henry Wood, Ouida and Marie Corelli. When I had washed and dressed, I pulled the curtains. There were the trees like peg-tops that I'd noticed when I arrived, but no sign of the sea—just flat fields. It didn't seem like an island at all, and disappointedly, I turned back to my room.

I noticed that the oilcloth on the floor was embossed

with pictures from *Struwwelpeter*, very worn in places but quite recognisable. There was poor Suck-a-Thumb and the Red-legged Scissor Man and that chubby lad Augustus and the boy with the long hair and nails. Sometimes there were holes in the pictures, and, to my dismay, I saw light filtering through and realised my bedroom was floored with openwork iron. I was lying on the floor, looking through a hole at the grey-and-white flagged hall below, when suddenly the door opened without anyone knocking, and I looked up to see Mrs. Gowley grinning at me. She carried a can of steaming water. " 'Ere's yer water, but I don't suppose yer want it now yer dressed, so it'll do for Mrs. Peebles." I felt ashamed of being seen by this horrible woman lying on the floor, and hurriedly got to my feet. As she left the room she told me breakfast would be ready in about half an hour. I thought, if she was going to get the breakfast, I might as well go outside and see what the back of the house was like, and perhaps get a glimpse of the sea.

I opened my bedroom door, and could hear Mrs. Gowley banging about in the upstairs kitchen. There was no sign of Mrs. Peebles. I walked down the landing trying not to make it clang too much, but the stairs made a terrible din; even when I reached the hall they were ringing. I looked at all the dark brown doors, but did not care to open them in case they contained Gowleys; there might have been a whole family of them for all I knew. At the end of the hall there was a stained-glass door with a coloured picture of William Shakespeare and parts of *As You Like It* were printed on the glass. I stood reading and admiring for a few minutes before opening it. Beyond was the skeleton of a large glass-less conservatory. It contained no flowers—just empty pots and dried-looking grape-vines that crawled over everything. There was another door leading into the garden.

When I went outside, the sun had just risen and it was very light. The garden was large and open, and beyond it lay the water, shimmering between the pine trees. Through a small fir plantation there was a narrow path. I followed it to the water. This is how I'd hoped the Island would be; but it was far more beautiful. The tide was not fully in and there were sea-gulls resting on the mud flats, and they were faintly blue from the sky. Across the water were the flat fields, with long grass gently blowing; and to my left was the open sea, with boats moving very slowly. I followed the path towards the sea. It led by an orchard of strange, old, misshapen trees, all overgrown with grey-green moss; but it became almost impass-able with reeds and overhanging trees, and I turned back. There was a wooden jetty built out into the water. Parts of it were missing; but I walked to the end to examine a small waterlogged dinghy that was moored there. Everything was very still and there was no sound at all except for the cry of seagulls and in the distance the occasional report from a gun.

I stood there overcome with peace and happiness, oblivious of the cold. Then I slowly turned towards the house. I noticed it appeared much lighter at the back than at the front, as if the stone it was built with had been bleached by sea and sun. A veranda ran across the lower part, and the winter remains of climbing flowers and bushes hung from the trellis-work. I entered the house the way I'd left, and started my first day as Mrs. Peebles's companion.

Mrs. Peebles was restrained and quiet that first day. I was later to learn that was how she usually was and the tears and confidences of the previous evening were comparatively rare. She was very polite and thoughtful towards me; but I could tell she found it an embarrassment having me with her all the time. She was glad to be able to give messages to the Gowleys through me, and, as she appeared never to leave the house, I did a certain amount of shopping for her. However, most of the tradesmen called at the house. She had very little interest in food, and I think before my arrival the Gowleys had taken advantage of this and she had been practically starved; but now I was there, her politeness and generosity demanded that I should be fed properly, and quite well-cooked, but badly served, meals appeared fairly frequently. Sometimes a dusty lid on a vegetable dish would cause Mrs. Peebles to rush from the room, sobbing with shame; but at other times she would eat from forks encrusted in stale egg-yolk, and apparently notice nothing wrong.

There was little enough for me to do, and I found it irked her if I kept asking, "What shall I do now?" I would do the mending sometimes, and make it last a long time, and I'd light the lamps when it was dusk and make the afternoon tea; but she was quite shocked when I suggested doing any cleaning. Mrs. Gowley's cleaning was a very sketchy kind of effort. It consisted of hanging about by the doors of whichever room we occupied, and sweeping all the dirt through the gratings on to the floor below, usually leaving it there. I discovered the Gowleys lived in all the old stone kitchens. The room that had been the dining-room, and the other ground floor rooms, were unused and almost empty, and echoed strangely when one entered them. They belonged now to damp and must, and sleepy ladybirds that had come in to escape the winter.

In the fir plantation there was an old gipsy caravan, which had once been painted brilliant colours, but had now faded to faint pinks and green. Gradually I made this caravan my own. I'd light the stove with fir-cones and bits of wood, and on sunny days I'd open the top half of the door and lean out and watch the sea. When it was cold or wet I'd pull down the bed and lie there dreaming and eating the apples I'd discovered in a green shed by the back door. Sometimes I'd read the schoolboys' stories from my bedroom. In the caravan there were books on veterinary subjects, but I found them depressing, the illustrations particularly, with their diagrams of calves' heads with water on the brain and hens' legs with bumble foot. I was glad my father hadn't had cases like that.

Once, as I lay there dreaming, Mrs. Gowley's flat face appeared over the door—flat and inquisitive, with steel spectacles above her upturned nose. She grinned, "It's nice to be some people and do nothing." If that had been said to me before I came to the Island, I'd have felt guilty and jumped to my feet; but now I lay relaxed and lazy and, without turning my head, drawled, "Well, you don't do very much yourself, do you?" The awful head started bobbing up and down, and for a moment I thought she was going to jump over the door, which I'd fortunately taken the precaution to bolt. "I like that! I must say, I like that—from you of all people! But you'll soon be slung out on your ear. You just wait until Mr. Peebles comes and finds how you 'ave neglected his mother! He chose us particular because he knew we was trust-worthy, and he'll listen to what we say—and that will be plenty!" The frightful head disappeared, and I heard her clumping down the steps, laughing in a false way, "Ha! Ha!" I laughed a real laugh, because I was sure I could persuade Blinkers to get rid of the Gowleys, and I remembered him telling me he had engaged them without even seeing them.

For a time I'd been puzzled when Mrs. Peebles referred to her trouble. I thought perhaps she meant her husband's death, or the house being burnt. But according to the Gowleys, she had tried to commit suicide a few years ago. She had been discovered by the bread man limply hanging in the green barn among the apples, and he had the presence of mind to cut her down with a pair of shears and untie the dreadful rope round her neck. Sometimes, when I looked at her there appeared to be a sinister brown stain round her neck, and I couldn't help wondering if her eyes had always been so prominent. Poor Mrs. Peebles, so sadly vague and harmless, they had wanted to shut her up in some home, but her son Henry had promised to be responsible for her and see that she never lived alone.

Sometimes, when I was in the caravan, I'd suddenly feel worried about her and run back to the house. There she would be, sitting gazing out of the window, but not looking. If she noticed me, she would say, "Yes, dear, what do you want?" and I'd say I'd come to make up the fire, or even to keep her company. But she never wanted company. Occasionally she would make an effort and become like a hostess. "Do sit down, dear. I'm afraid it must be very dull for you here. I don't know any young people, you see; but my son Henry will be home for Christmas and you will be able to enjoy yourselves then. It won't be long to wait. Perhaps you would like to play a game of cards— whist, for instance . . . There is a pack of cards in a shell box somewhere—on the davenport, I think." I'd find the cards and we would solemnly play whist together in the fading afternoon light, but the effort of concentration would be too much for her, and big tears would come splashing down on the cards and the game would end.

Stored away in the back of Mrs. Peebles's mind were facts that she had almost learnt by heart. She would rattle off the names and habits of hundreds of different kinds of insects, or, it might be, the population and names of various states in India. Sometimes she would describe ancient cults and religions, and I enjoyed listening to her; but she usually broke off and forgot what she was talking about when she reached the most interesting part.

The days had a dreamlike quality on the Island and slowly drifted past. It was a shock when something from the outside world tore a hole in the misty peace-fulness. I think it must have been about three weeks after my arrival that I received a letter from Mrs. Churchill. It filled me with contrition because I had never even bothered to send her a postcard to say I'd arrived safely. I held the pink envelope in my hand for a few minutes before I could force myself to read it and bring the ugliness of the home I'd left into my present dreamy life. I sat on the dining-room window-sill with my back turned to the creek, slowly tore open the envelope, and read:

"My dear Girl,

"I am sorry not to have heard from you and hope all is well as it is here at present. I think your Father is drinking quite a lot although he doesn't say any-thing to me, but sometimes I think he talks to him-self. He doesn't see that Rosa Fisher no more because she is in hospital and is real bad so I hear. You can't help feeling sorry for her in a way.

"My poor old Nell died, the stout black and white one, and the vet said I'd killed her with kindness, so I don't feel so bad about it. The swiss rolls that dog had. Although it's so late in the year there are still chrysanthemums in my garden and my holly bush is having berries this year.

"I saw your young friend that is dumb and I must

say she was a bit overdone. I'm surprised her mother allows it. You wouldn't think she was dumb to look at her now.

"Well, dear, I must close now, and please write and let me know how you are getting on. Vera joins in sending her love.

Yours,

A. Churchill."

I thought of my father 'talking to himself' and 'drinking quite a lot' and remembered the stumbling footsteps that passed my bedroom door sometimes in the night. I thought of Mrs. Churchill's hot, hot room and the two fat panting dogs.

Then I remembered how I'd floated up to the ceiling and broken the gas mantle. Could it really have happened? Something similar had happened my first night on the Island, but I hadn't seemed to go so high that time—perhaps because I'd laughed. Could it be a thing that happened to people when they slept in different beds? Perhaps it was something that often happened to people but was never mentioned, like piles—I'd seen an advertisement "Why suffer in silence?"—but they were rude things, most likely, and floating would be rather nice when one became used to it.

I looked at Mrs. Churchill's letter again and read

about Rosa being in hospital. I remembered leaving her in the dusk with her dreadful cough, and felt I should have been kinder. That sad clown's face and her greedy grasping at gaiety—and now she would wear a sad clown's face all the time, except perhaps when the doctors came round the ward. I wondered what Mrs. Churchill meant about Lucy being 'overdone'. Could it be the powder on her face or the doorknocker hair-style? "Lucy, don't change!" I whispered. "Be the gentle, speechless Lucy you used to be, with your green-white face and your hair pouring down your back."

I answered Mrs. Churchill's letter immediately because I felt, once I'd posted it, home would be very far away again; it might be weeks before I received another letter. When I had written my letter, I had to go nearly a mile down the lane to post it. The wind blew in the tops of the trees and the last of the leaves came sailing down. Strange white hens were scratching in a hedge, very fat, with feathers all down their legs. A man standing by a shed sharpening a scythe said they were called white Cochin hens and were very tame and so heavy they couldn't fly. I went close to one and stroked its feathers. It stayed quite still; only its eyes in its over-small head flickered. The man said, "They aren't good eaters—Cochins; the fat's in the wrong places. Look at that, now!" and he pointed to a bloated hen's body hanging from the shed. It was quite bare except for a few feathers on its head, and between its relaxed beak there was one crystal bead of water. I looked at the pitiful and obscene sight and found myself thinking of Mrs. Peebles hanging in the barn—but at least she was thin and had clothes on her body. I turned away, but said "Good morning" to the man quite politely. After all, he was so used to hens' bodies he didn't realise how depressing one could look, so fat and pale and gently swinging in the wind.

At the top of the lane I met a man leading an enormous horse with a great arched neck and ribbons entwined in its mane. A pretty young woman who was also posting a letter, said, "Ah, that's Finstal Rhyman—the stallion. He visits the Island every year," and she left me and went to speak to the man. Evidently they were old friends, because they were soon laughing and talking to each other, while the beautiful horse stood powerful and proud, with the sun and wind and changing light rippling on him.

I crossed the road to a cottage where one could buy vegetables, and the woman asked me in to have a cup of tea while her husband went to the barn to collect the onions and marrow I needed. We sat in her over-crowded kitchen and drank strong tea with condensed milk in it and discussed her baby. It lay in a wicker cradle by the range, and all the time we were talking its large and incredibly blue eyes followed a group of flies that circled and danced near the ceiling. Its mother looked up, too, and said, "The flies are late this year, but the frost will take them." The man came in with my vegetables. The marrow was fat and already turning golden. When I left the kitchen the whole family were all gazing upwards at the dancing flies.

Chapter Fourteen

IT WAS ALMOST CHRISTMAS before the frost came. The water in the cart tracks turned to very white ice, which I enjoyed crunching with my feet, and the pond at the top of the lane was frozen with thin ice which the village children called 'cat ice', but which remained so thin I don't think it would even have borne the weight of a cat. In the early morning, when I looked out of my bedroom window, the trees and fields were white with hoar frost and the glass in the window was beautifully patterned with it. I'd never loved the frost before but now it enchanted me. Besides the beauty, there were the sounds: the snap of a stick, the hard rustle of a frozen leaf, the crack of breaking ice—even the birds' winter cries seemed to be sharp and intensified.

Blinkers came home for a few days at Christmas. It was a happy time for us all. Even Mrs. Peebles became almost gay—she was so pleased to have her son home. The three of us cooked the Christmas dinner together and gave the Gowleys a day off. I was delighted to see their square and ugly backs retreating down the path between the peg-top trees, Mrs. Gowley walking, as always, a few paces behind her husband. They didn't return until the following day. One lens of Mrs. Gowley's spectacles was cracked, and Mr. Gowley had a black eye.

Blinkers tried to persuade his mother to come for a walk with us, but she utterly refused to leave the house or even to come downstairs. All the same, she was very cheerful and very pleased with the presents he had given her, and talked to him quite reasonably about the practice he was taking over in Earl's Court. She even agreed that perhaps she might later on come and live with him there. We all knew this was very unlikely, but it made them both happy to talk about it.

On Blinkers's last day we went for a long walk together, right to the deserted seashore. The icy wind blew in our faces until they felt quite stiff, but when we turned our backs to the sea, we seemed to be tingling with warmth. I found a dead sea-bird with glowing green legs and buried it in the sand dunes, and, as I stood on its grave, looking out to sea, I could see a misty island, which Blinkers said was the Isle of Wight. On our way home we walked through some waste land. There were people skating on a stretch of frozen water. Some could hardly skate at all, and had brooms and even chairs to support them; but others were gracefully curling and curving, and there was one dapper little man who skated better than anyone, although he had a tiny girl—almost a baby—sitting on one of his boots and clutching his leg. Above the skaters sea-gulls circled and cried, and round the water there were boots and shoes in isolated pairs. Boys with iron-studded boots cut great white lines in the ice as they made slides (they called them Roman candles) and sometimes sparks came. Bewildered dogs ran about madly barking and trying to find their owners. We walked on to the ice. I could feel it vibrating as the skaters flew past us, sometimes several holding hands and laughing. Although I was not alone, I felt lonely, and wished I was part of the skating, not just watching it.

Darkness began to come and we left the ice and walked through the narrow roads to Mrs. Peebles's house. Henry held my arm. I knew it gave him great pleasure to hold my arm like that, but it meant nothing to me; I'd rather have walked by myself.

As we walked, I asked him if it was usual for people to sometimes rise into the air when they were resting in their beds—particularly in strange beds. I asked him this because it was dark and it was easier to say something that worried me in the darkness like that. It seemed very unlikely that Henry floated about his bedroom at night—he must have weighed about fourteen stone—but he might have friends that often did this kind of thing and talked about it freely. He was very slow in understanding what I meant. That was the sort of thing that exasperated me about him—his slowness. When he did understand what I was trying to tell him, he said most emphatically that no one ever left their beds and floated to the ceiling, but they might think they had done so in a dream or if they were light-headed or delirious. I thought that sounded quite reasonable: if you were light-headed, you would feel that you had no weight at all and were floating around. But at the time my floating had seemed real enough and I remembered the powdery broken gas mantle. He didn't seem to like me talking about floating, so the subject was changed, and we spoke of his house in Earl's Court and all its great empty rooms.

As we turned into his mother's road, we could just distinguish the forms of Mr. and Mrs. Gowley stumping along, Mr. Gowley leading, as usual, and carrying a ladder. They looked guilty—like housebreakers returning from the job. They grunted a surly "Evening!" and we left them behind.

The following morning, before he left for London, Blinkers gave me a skating lesson on the pond at the top of the road. I wore a pair of Mrs. Peebles's pointed boots and some rusty skates that Blinkers had discovered in the shed. The boots had been green with mould—rather beautiful they had looked, so green and pointed—but now they were a shiny black against the dark ice, which cracked and wheezed as Blinkers dragged me across its surface. Ducks' unblinking eyes watched us from the bank—already the hole that someone had made for them in the ice had frozen over again. Blinkers was a very patient teacher, but I didn't get very far that first skating lesson. I seemed to skate rather like a Japanese, with tiny, stiff movements. However, I did learn how to fall without hurting myself, and in the afternoon I went back to the pond and, with the aid of a broom, managed to get round in my stiff and careful way. I was scared away eventually by a mob of shouting schoolboys, who rushed about the ice, sliding and yelling, "Look at Miss trying to skate."

I hurried home to light the lamps. Mrs. Peebles was crying to herself in the darkness because her son had gone. I tried to comfort her with buttered toast and gentle words, and eventually we sat beside the fire playing dominoes, while tears very slowly dripped down Mrs. Peebles's withered cheeks.

The following day a widow from Portsmouth came to lunch, and we ate minced turkey and drank the remains of the Christmas port wine. Mrs. Peebles was in a state of great excitement about this visitor, a visitor being a very rare event in her life; but I knew that by the evening she would be in a terrible state of exhaustion and would creep to her bed shivering and crying. It was always like this if her day varied in the slightest.

After lunch she waved me away. I left the widows either side of the fire talking about a dance that occurred on a ship twenty years ago—two black figures living in the past, though at least Mrs. Peebles had her son.

Under a winter sun I ran to the waste ground with my skates under each arm. I feared the ice might have melted, but even in the distance I could hear the sound of skates cutting the ice and voices that carried sharp and clear in the winter air. When I reached the skaters I saw the ice had melted a lot round the edges. I felt rather frightened trying to get on to it without falling in the water. Also, I had been too proud to take my broom, and found it almost impossible to go round without its aid. Two enormous schoolgirl sisters, looking even bigger than they really were because of the height given them by their skates, came to my assistance. They each took one of my hands and pulled me round. I was too scared to move my legs at all, and just kept my feet together. They gave me much advice, followed by a hearty push in the back that sent me spinning across the ice. Then they deserted me.

I landed at the feet of a young man wearing a white sweater. He picked me up with much care, as if I'd been a little wax dolly, and carefully brushed my coat with his hands. I thanked him, but I could hardly bear to look at him, he was so handsome. There was a sort of aura of easy happiness around him; no one else I'd seen close-to had that look about them. He spoke, but I could only hear the sea-gulls crying as they circled overhead. Then somehow we were skimming over the ice together and I wasn't nervous. I only had a feeling of exaltation. The frost was on our faces, and it seemed as if we were the only people there. In an incredibly short time the afternoon had gone and I was sitting on the beautiful young man's coat while he unlaced my boots. When one of my feet was free, he encircled my ankle with the fingers of one of his hands, and I was glad they were so slim.

Together we left the frozen waste land. Instead of returning to Mrs. Peebles we walked in the church-yard under the yew trees. He told me his name was Nicholas and he was on leave from the Navy and was staying with his parents, who lived on the Island near the golf course. He said his father was a doctor. In return, I told him my father was a vet and all kinds of animals lived in our house. I also told him I came from London, because I thought that sounded rather good; but he said, "Yes, I can tell that from the way you speak, my dear little Cockney." Indignantly I insisted I wasn't a Cockney, "I've never even heard Bow bells, and I've been to a private school, and if I had an accent of any kind, it would be a Welsh one," but he still seemed to think I was a Cockney, which hurt me very much, and I said it was time to return to Mrs. Peebles and light the lamps. However, happiness soon came back because he seemed to want to see me again so much, even if I had a Cockney accent, and we arranged to meet at the frozen water. He insisted that it would still be frozen and waiting there for us, and that even the sides that had melted would be frozen again.

We said good-bye outside the church. I think I hoped he would kiss me, but he only put his arm round me for a moment. Then he suddenly started laughing at a gravestone that loomed in the near darkness. I'd often seen it before and admired it, but this church-yard was unknown to him. He stood in front of the marble arm-chair laughing, and, to my horror, even tried to sit on it. Then he struck a match and read the inscription, "Mother, at rest at last," and laughed so much that I was laughing, too.

All the morning as I helped Mrs. Peebles polish silver, she talked about her friend's visit the previous day, "Just think of it, dear: we both became engaged to our husbands the same day, and later on it was whitlows that we had, both on the same day. They had to be lanced and I seem to remember I lost my nail —so unpleasant!" But all the time I was thinking, 'Will he be there? Oh, will I see him again?' In the house it felt very cold. I had no chance to go outside to see if the ice still held, but from the windows everything looked frozen stiff and very still.

We ate boiled mutton and sauce with capers in it. The afternoon had almost come, and when Mrs. Gowley had cleared away the remains of our meal, I almost shooed Mrs. Peebles to her fireside chair, where I hoped she would sit and doze away the afternoon. But she unexpectedly fussed and fretted and refused to sit down, and stood by the window, fidgeting with the blindcord. Then I said, "What would you like to do this afternoon?" She replied, "I don't know; it seems very dull," and tears welled up in her eyes. "Couldn't we play Snap?" she added, in a more hopeful voice. I thought, 'Why should I spend the afternoon playing with a half-witted old woman when I could be flying across the ice with Nicholas?' Then I suggested that she wrote a letter to her son. If she wrote it that afternoon I could post it after tea. She could tell him all about her friend coming to lunch and how they had been girls together and about their whitlows; he'd be so glad to receive a letter from her so soon. "Yes, that is a good idea," she agreed, and went towards her writing-table. "But there isn't any ink. I'm sure we haven't any in the house." I reassured her on that point and arranged paper and envelopes on her blotter and then exclaimed over the absence of stamps and suggested going to the village for some. "And you wouldn't mind if I just watched the skating for a few minutes, would you?" No, she wouldn't mind. She had suddenly become interested in writing her letter because she had discovered in her writing-drawer a long-forgotten pen—the handle made from a long, vivid blue feather. So I left her there writing, and on my way to the frozen waste land even remembered to buy some stamps. I felt so grateful for my freedom.

The ice was still there and, just as Nicholas had said, it was better than ever; even the sides were frozen again. There were not many people on it that afternoon. In the distance I could see Nicholas in his white sweater, skating by himself and looking for me, and my heart sort of melted and turned over and tears came into my eyes—he was so gleaming and beautiful. I wondered if he felt like that about me. Then I remembered how he had called me a Cockney. Of course, he didn't think of me as a goddess, or anything like that; he just rather liked me, and I amused him. So, when he came to me, I was feeling sad and humble. But, when he helped me on with my skates, I became like a queen, and so I was for the rest of the afternoon. We couldn't skate for very long, so he walked home with me. In Mrs. Peebles's lane he put his arm round me, and once he pressed his face against mine so that the sides of our faces touched. It was only for a moment, but then I knew what the word rapture meant.

Chapter Fifteen

THE SLEET CAME. It turned to rain, which washed away most of the ice, and what remained lay inches under water. In spite of the sleet I walked to the waste ground. It now looked a wretched sort of place. I went there again in the rain. But there was no sign of Nicholas; it was utterly deserted. On the draggled, wet grass there were scattered chestnut-shells, all that remained of the skaters, and I remembered how we had bought chestnuts from the old man with a brazier and I'd dropped one on the ice and a little hole had come.

On the third day I thought, 'I'll never see him again now. His leave will be over and he will be back in Portsmouth.' Nevertheless, I walked towards the waste ground. A golden winter sun lit up the hedges and I thought, 'I expect that is what Moses saw—a bright patch of sun on a hedge—and he thought it was a holy fire.' When I came to the end of Mrs. Peebles's road, I saw Nicholas standing with his hands in his pockets, alone and bored. To see him suddenly and unexpectedly like that so filled me with happiness I almost stumbled towards him. He greeted me quite casually. He had waited at the end of the road, he said, in the hope of seeing me. He was on his way to a boat-building yard near-by and thought I'd like to come along. I readily agreed, although I knew and cared nothing about boats—in fact, I'd never been in one. So we went to the yard which was on the creek. I'd often noticed some black sheds and boats, but never realised the boats were actually being made there. It was a kind of boat factory. There was a heavenly smell of wood, and men were working on the hulls of several small sailing-boats, and there were larger boats being repaired. I'd never realised how deep the hulls of boats were before, or how graceful and beautiful they were. I hung about the sheds while Nicholas talked and laughed with the men and asked their advice about a sailing-boat he intended to build. His fair hair fell over one eye, and I noticed that, although he was so hand-some, his nose wasn't quite straight, and for some reason it made me even more enchanted with him.

The afternoon lasted such a short time. It was terrible to have to return to Mrs. Peebles when I could have been with Nicholas. I always seemed to be saying good-bye to him: sometimes two days would pass and I wouldn't see him at all, and they were wasted days.

Once, when I came to the end of the road hoping to see him, all I saw was a grey car. But, when I looked again, I saw Nicholas was at the wheel. We spent the afternoon driving round the Island; it was simply wonderful, quite different to the drive in the pony and trap with Blinkers. Then there was the day I went to Nicholas's home. He wanted to show me the boat he was building in a shed on the beach. It was just the skeleton of a very small sailing-boat, and it didn't mean much to me except that it had been made by Nicholas. But I looked interested and kept saying, "Umph" every now and then, and that did very well. He showed me the canvas for the sails and asked if I'd sew them for him if he cut them out in a week or two. Of course, I agreed. I couldn't help wondering what Mrs. Peebles would think when I sat down to sew an enormous piece of canvas, and how horribly stiff canvas was; but it would be an honour to sew for Nicholas.

When Nicholas could drag himself away from the shed, we walked through his garden to his house. We went in through the kitchens, passing two white-capped and aproned maids, sewing at a long table. The main part of the house was unlike anything I'd ever seen before: light polished floors and Oriental rugs, blazing log fires, and the most comfortable chairs I'd ever sat in, upholstered in flowered chintz. It was unutterably grand, and yet there were just plain painted walls, no wallpaper, only one picture over the fire-place, and hardly any ornaments. Everything in the house was strange and wonderful to me. The maids brought us tea and placed it on a low table by the fire, and we sat together on a sofa. I poured out from a silver teapot. The sugar-bowl and milk-jug were silver, too. Nicholas said it was rotten old silver an uncle had brought home from India and the only way to keep it clean was to boil it once a week. We ate scones and jam before that blazing fire, and I pretended to myself that we were married and this was our home.

Then Nicholas's mother returned. She stood, tall and easy, in her drawing-room, taking off her gloves. Nicholas introduced us, and she did not seem to be surprised to find a stranger guest in her home.

"Ring the bell for more tea, darling," she cried to Nicholas, as she lifted the lid of the teapot and peered inside. "This looks revolting." She threw her coat and little hat on a chair and sat in another, and, to my amazement, asked her son for a cigarette. She sat there looking at us through her cigarette-smoke and flicking the ash in the fire-grate while she waited for her tea. Somehow I managed to stand up and tell them I must return home. Nicholas's mother said, "Must you really? Do come another time," but I knew that as soon as I left the room she would completely forget me. I left as the maid came with the fresh tea. Nicholas walked to the garden gate with me. He just said, "You will be able to find your way home, won't you?" and gave my arm an affectionate pat and returned to the house. I heard the front door slam.

I partly walked and partly ran home in the darkness. I knew I was very late and poor Mrs. Peebles would have had to struggle with the lamps by herself. Perhaps she was sitting crying in the dark over the dying fire. When I returned, she had managed to light the lamp, but the fire had gone out, and, of course, she had had no tea. For the first time since I'd known her she was annoyed with me. She didn't rail and rant, but was very distant and cold, and I knew I deserved it. As I lit the fire and drew it up with news-paper, I found I was shaking. I suddenly felt utterly miserable, although I'd been so happy before.

I stayed with Mrs. Peebles the next afternoon. She didn't really want me—she just went to sleep—but at least I was there to get her tea and I was forgiven. When I went to the kitchen to make tea, Mrs. Gowley must have heard me clanking down the passage. I heard a noise on the stairs and then her goblin-like face peered round the door. "So yer getting the lady's tea, are you?" she said as she leered at me through her spectacles. "Out with your chap yesterday afternoon, weren't yer? Mr. Peebles wouldn't like his mother neglected while you fool about with a chap in a garden shed. You may not think it, but Mr. Gowley saw you both going into that shed yesterday afternoon. Gave him quite a shock it did." I felt a bit sick and afraid, but only for a moment; then I remembered how Nicholas's mother had spoken to the servants. I managed to say, "That will do, Mrs. Gowley, you can go downstairs." She looked startled, and the blood slowly mounted to her face. Then she shouted, "I like that from you. Who do yer think yer are, anyway? You make me laugh." And, pretending to laugh in an awful 'ho! ho!' way, she left the room.

A day or two later I was in the garden, looking at the crumpled primrose leaves and hoping to see some buds, as I'd heard they were early on the Island, particularly the purple ones. There seemed to be spring in the air, and on the mud flats the sandpipers were making their strange cry. Then I heard steps behind me. They belonged to Mr. Gowley. He came right up to me and looked at me out of his frightful eyes that moved independently.

"Well, Alice, I haven't had the chance to speak to you for a long time. You're a dark horse, an' no mistake, but we won't say any more about that. The missus and I are a bit behind with the payments for my poor old dad's keep and I wondered if you'd like to help us a bit. A quid or something like that would make all the difference to the old boy." He came close to me, grinning and showing his yellow, uneven teeth. I felt terribly afraid, afraid of the evilness that was about him. For a moment I stood there, breaking a piece of stick that was in my hand, then I turned and walked very stiffly away, and, although it was cold, sweat was coming from me.

I went back to the house to think. Mrs. Peebles sat beside me, sorting out buttons and rather fretfully complaining that she was sure she had had a set of blue ones and the cut steel ones were missing, too. As I watched her fussing over the stupid buttons, I began to feel calmer. I knew that there was no real reason to be afraid of the Gowleys. They couldn't really harm me: the most they could do would be to write a spiteful letter to Blinkers—and, surely, he wouldn't believe anything they said. He had already made up his mind to get rid of them as soon as the spring came and it wasn't so difficult to get people to work in the house, although it was isolated. The spring was almost here now, and the Gowleys would be gone. I could imagine them muttering and cursing as they walked down the drive carrying their bursting cardboard cases, one in front of the other.

I wrote a letter to Blinkers. It was a great effort to do so, but I wanted to be on the safe side. I told him the Gowleys had been even more unpleasant than usual and Mr. Gowley had tried to blackmail me, if you could call it blackmail; and I told him I'd been skating with a sailor called Nicholas and spent an afternoon watching him making a boat in a shed, and I hoped he wouldn't mind and think I'd been neglecting his mother. I really felt guilty about neglecting Mrs. Peebles, and I didn't want him to know how much she had been alone.

The next afternoon she was alone again. Nicholas suddenly arrived in his father's motor-car and drove right up to the house. I was in the back garden. As soon as I heard the noise of the engine, I knew it must be him and ran round to the front. There he stood on the doorstep, tugging at the bell and looking very handsome in his huge motoring coat. It was his last day's leave, and he wanted me to go for a drive with him. I rushed upstairs and asked Mrs. Peebles if she would mind my going. She didn't mind in the least; she was really excited about the car and almost ran to the kitchen window so that she could see it. I put on my outdoor things and hurried downstairs to find Nicholas doing something to the car and both the Gowleys dancing about on the doorstep. I was just in time to hear Mr. Gowley's cheeky voice saying, "Er, who told you you could bring that thing 'ere?" Nicholas completely ignored him, but I could feel the blood mounting in my face and tears coming to my eyes.

Nicholas said, "Oh, hallo, you were quick," and, for the Gowleys' benefit, I said, "Oh yes, Mrs. Peebles didn't mind me coming at all." Then he opened the car door for me and, when I was seated, I looked up at the window and waved to Mrs. Peebles, and she waved back. We drove away, leaving a great pool of oil, and then we had our golden afternoon—at least, it was golden to me.

Chapter Sixteen

THEN NICHOLAS HAD GONE and I went back into my dreaming, lonely life. I spent hours in the caravan, sometimes reading and at other times just thinking about Nicholas—his laughing blue eyes and the fair flop of hair across his forehead; the way he slightly turned his toes in when he was sitting down, and the back of his neck, so clean and somehow defenceless. I remembered how I'd cried myself to sleep the night he left the Island, although we parted in such happiness and he expected to be home again soon. But I couldn't bear to know that it was certain that I wouldn't be seeing him the following day, that there was nothing to look forward to perhaps for weeks.

And then in the night it happened again and I was floating, definitely floating. The moonlight was streaming whitely through the window, and I could see the curtains gently flapping in the night wind. I'd left my bed, and except for a sheet, the clothes lay scattered on the floor. I gently floated about the room.

Sometimes I went very close to the ceiling, but I wouldn't touch it in case it made me fall to the ground. If I came near to an object—a wall, or the tall wardrobe, for instance—some sixth sense seemed to steer me away, rather as I've heard it does with bats, and the feeling that this was so gave me confidence. Somehow I knew I must keep myself quite straight, yet relaxed. I floated horizontally, feet first, but was relieved to notice that the window was only partly open and there was no danger of floating away into the night.

I don't know how long I remained in the air like that; I should imagine about seven minutes. Then I can remember a feeling of great exhaustion stealing over me, and a longing for my bed. I willed myself down to it and it happened quite gently: one moment there was nothing beneath me but air, and then I felt my still warm mattress. I lay there almost fainting with tiredness before I could creep out and collect the blankets. Then a deep and dreamless sleep enveloped me.

I awoke to the sound of Mrs. Gowley clanking past my door. I felt so tired it seemed almost impossible to leave my bed; but, when I did and leant out of my window and felt the early spring sun on my face, I felt refreshed. I watched sea-gulls circling round an old man who was ploughing, and somebody's hens pecking in the hedge in our garden. In the distance there was the sound of ducks and I felt a strange homesickness for no home I'd known.

While we ate our breakfast and drank the rather good coffee Mrs. Gowley unexpectedly made, we hardly spoke a word. I kept thinking about my experiences of the night. I knew now that Blinkers was wrong about my being light-headed and it had really happened. Probably it happened to hundreds of people, but was never spoken about. I thought I'd try Mrs. Peebles—nothing really surprised her much, poor thing! So I said, "Mrs. Peebles," but there was no answer—she just crunched a little piece of egg-shell that had somehow got in her mouth.

"Mrs. Peebles," I said, much louder, and she looked at me in her half-dazed way, "Mrs. Peebles, have you ever heard of anyone floating about their rooms—leaving the ground, I mean, and just floating about?"

She bit her egg-shell thoughtfully. Then her face brightened, and she said, "Yes, levitation I expect you mean. It used to be quite common, I believe, at one time, but I can't remember when. There was a monk I seem to remember hearing about called some name like Joseph of Cupertino, or is that the name of a place in Italy? This man used to behave most strangely, and was not allowed to sing in the choir because he used to rise up and remain suspended in the air and caused quite a sensation and upset the service. This went on for many years, and the poor monk had to remain in his room, where a private chapel was arranged for him. I heard he fasted and practised mortification, but to no avail. Poor man! it was quite an embarrassment for him! My mother used to tell of a man called Home, who was taken up by some society gentlemen. He floated in and out of the windows of some big house in London—Ashley House, I think it was. One doesn't hear about that kind of thing now."

I listened fascinated. So it was true: I did float, or levitate, or whatever it was.

"Mrs. Peebles," I asked, "have you ever floated?"

She looked quite annoyed. "Oh no, I wouldn't do a thing like that. I'm not peculiar."

She went back to crunching her egg-shell, which seemed to last a long time, and I returned to my thinking. It was quite plain that some people floated—not everyone, about as many as were left-handed, perhaps —but it was peculiar and not a thing to boast about, just something to keep to yourself and practise when no one was about. I wondered if it could occur in the daytime, or outside. It would be wonderful to float in a wood among birds if one didn't bump into the trees and become entangled in their branches.

I was thinking about these things when Mrs. Peebles suddenly jumped up from the table and said the

Gowleys were trying to poison her, she was quite sure of it. I had to take her to her room quickly so that she wouldn't encounter Mrs. Gowley when she came to clear away and accuse her of all kind of horrors. Sometimes this happened and it was frightening; Mrs. Peebles wildly crying and the Gowleys threatening and bullying the poor demented creature. They shouted about being treated with fairness and the police and witnesses, pretending that they took her accusations seriously. Then she would appeal to me and I'd become involved, and all the Gowleys' vehemence would be turned on me. They were repulsive people.

Fortunately, I managed to get Mrs. Peebles into the drawing-room just before Mrs. Gowley appeared with some letters. There was one for me from Blinkers; there was also one for his mother, which calmed her down a little. My letter was an answer to the one I'd sent complaining about the Gowleys. The envelope had been tampered with, and, when I looked at the postmark, I saw they had kept it back a day. There wasn't much in the letter except kindness and affection, and an assurance that he would sack the offensive Gowleys. He already had someone else in view—a married couple who would be free at Easter, a superior kind of people with a little girl. He didn't say a word of reproach about Nicholas—he said he was grateful to him for teaching me to skate. He was going to be home for Easter and would dismiss the Gowleys then, as he wanted to be in the house when they left to make sure they didn't take anything that did not belong to them. He also told his mother that the Gowleys would soon be leaving. She became wildly happy and declared that, as soon as they left, she would be able to go downstairs and sit in the garden and perhaps even do some gardening—things she had given up years before the Gowleys came to live with her.

In the afternoon I left her sitting by the window, watching the incoming tide and enjoying the warmth of the sun through the glass. It was a lovely spring day, with clouds racing across the sky. A faint, fresh greenness was showing. The leaf buds on the trees were swollen and arrow-headed, and in the hedges catkins were blowing, like animated caterpillars. I passed the old man who bred Cochin hens. He said, "Come and look, Missy." In his shed was a great, puffed out white hen, and every now and then a minute chicken would appear from under her wings. "They are the first chickens to be born on the Island this year, I shouldn't wonder," he said with pride, and shame kept me from admitting they were the first baby chickens I could remember seeing. The old man bent down to adjust the string he wore tied round his legs below his knees, most likely to make his trousers more comfortable. It took him some time to straighten up again because his back had so much rheumatism in it. When I left, he was grinding some corn very fine for the chickens' first meal, and I was quite forgotten.

I walked to the church on a day of soft wind and cloud and sun. I stood by the stone arm-chair with 'At rest at last' engraved upon it, but I couldn't admire it any longer. It was something to be laughed at and there was no one to laugh with.

It was lonely there under the sighing yew trees, and I left the churchyard and walked in the sun. Two riders were coming towards me. They cantered past on the grass verge without seeing me, the girl leading. The man who rode behind was Nicholas. They passed high above me, with the changing sun shining on their chestnut horses, and I thought, 'They are the lordly ones; they are so beautiful and free up there.' Even the faint squeak of their harness as they passed sounded proud.

I watched them riding towards the sea, then I walked to a small wood that I knew well. In a clearing there was a felled beech tree, where I often sat so still that birds came quite near. Now I lay down on this tree and felt a lonely sadness coming over me in waves. Slow tears ran from my eyes and trickled into my ears. I thought, 'I even cry in a humble, common way, with tears flowing into my ears.' But the humble, common tears had relieved me, and I began to hope that perhaps

Nicholas had only returned to the Island that day and the lovely girl was a cousin or a childhood friend. To-morrow he would be at Mrs. Peebles's house, perhaps in his father's car; or he might bring me the sails of his boat to sew.

I almost believed this would happen, but not quite. Then I comforted myself with the knowledge that at least I wasn't earthbound like most people. I lay there on the felled tree completely relaxed, and tried to will myself to float. I lay there and nothing happened, but I felt drowsy and limp and light. Then I rose in the air, only a few feet. All the noises of the wood ceased, and there was a great silence as if from shock at all the laws of Nature being broken. I became afraid, so afraid I became all rigid. Then suddenly I was down on the grass, rather shaken but quite unhurt. I felt a small thrill of triumph. I could float when I wanted to; it wasn't a dream or illness. I really could levitate myself. Walking home in the fading afternoon, I felt a new pride.

Chapter Seventeen

THE DAY AFTER my experience in the wood began badly. No hot water was brought to my room, and only weak, cold tea and toast appeared on the break-fast-table. Mrs. Gowley sniffed and snorted as she cleared away the meagre meal, and I knew I was in disgrace. Perhaps they had received a letter from Blinkers dismissing them. At lunch-time cold food was banged on the table. I was thankful to see Mrs. Peebles was in one of her dreaming moods, unnoticing and withdrawn into herself. In the afternoon I left her sitting in the big window overlooking the creek. She was vaguely sorting out her buttons, and raised no objection to my leaving her, although it was later than I usually took my walk. I'd been faintly hoping Nicholas would call; but now I was all impatient to be gone in case he was waiting at the end of the road.

There was no one there except a small boy fishing in the pond. He wore a shawl pinned over his head, and, when he turned towards me, I saw his face was swollen with mumps or toothache. I asked him if he'd seen a gentleman pass that way, walking, or perhaps in a motor-car. Adjusting his shawl, he gave me a vacant look and said, "I don't know. I've got a kernel in me throat." Then he turned his back on me and resumed his fishing. I walked to the waste ground, but that was deserted too—even the flood water had gone. And then, although I hadn't planned it, I was walking towards the dunes that lay behind Nicholas's home.

I trudged along with the wind blowing in my face. A man passed me on a horse, but it wasn't Nicholas. I followed the hoof marks in the sand, looking down at them all the time until I heard voices coming through the wind. Then I looked up. I could see Nicholas bending over a boat, painting it maybe. He was wearing a fisherman's jersey, just a common thing, and there was tar or something like it streaked across his forehead, but he looked resplendent and I felt as if I were melting in wonder at seeing him there before me. I stood quite still, and then I heard a girl's voice. I turned towards it. There was the riding girl. Her hair was the colour of dying golden-rod and burnished by the sun; it was uncovered and blowing in the wind. Her blouse was undone at the neck, and round her shoulders she or Nicholas had draped his jacket. She was sitting on an upturned bucket with as much grace as if it had been a throne, it seemed to me, and I saw she was actually smoking a cigarette. She said something to Nicholas in her easy, laughing way. Her head was tilted back and her lovely neck was flowing out of her open blouse.

I stood there watching. I tried to think, 'Why, they are dressed like a couple of tramps!' But I knew that even in those careless clothes they had a radiant grace. I couldn't bring myself to come nearer. I turned away, and after walking a few steps, I found myself running towards Mrs. Peebles's house.

I arrived home breathless. All the doors of the house were open as if a great wind had been blowing through it and now everything was still. Mrs. Peebles's voice, sad and lost, was calling to me, and, as my footsteps rang on the metal stairs, the landing rang with hers. She was crying.

"Alice, they have gone. The Gowleys have gone without a word! What will my son say?"

I tried to comfort her. I told her they had probably gone out for the afternoon, and if they had really left, it was a very good thing; and I reminded her how much she disliked them. But she had the idea fixed in her mind that her son would be angry with her.

I went downstairs and opened the Gowleys' dirty doors. Empty bottles and mouse-eaten bread everywhere, old newspapers and grease—but no Gowleys. I gave the boiler some attention and opened the windows to let some of the smell away. Then I heard Mrs. Peebles screaming. The screams came from the dining-room and there she stood, pointing to the mantelpiece. It looked all right to me, except that the wallpaper was a brighter shade in one place. Then I saw that something large was missing: the gilt clock with the cupid on top wasn't there any more. Also, the silver candle-sticks had gone from the sideboard. Together we opened the silver drawer. All that was there was bright green baize; no silver. Mrs. Peebles had stopped screaming. Now she was shaking and jerking like a poor old·puppet. I suggested going into the village to fetch a policeman, but she wouldn't let me. "It was a policeman that they fetched before; I don't want people to see the police coming to the house again. But what will Henry say? His father's clock and silver all gone—all gone."

Eventually I got her to bed. By that time I felt almost dead with worry and tiredness, and was dreading the responsibility of looking after Mrs. Peebles on my own. Before I went to bed I managed to scribble a note to Blinkers asking him to come quickly and telling him about the Gowleys' departure with the silver. I was too tired to post it that night. I decided to give it to the milkman to post in the morning.

I awoke with a great weight on my mind. I went straight to Mrs. Peebles's room to see if she needed anything. She lay there very quiet and remote and, in her strange way, rather beautiful. She refused breakfast in bed, and we ate a silent meal together. She seemed stunned. There was a silence over the house, with no Gowleys and Mrs. Peebles sitting so quietly on the drawing-room sofa. She sat very straight and her eyes were wide open; but she was looking at nothing. I did not like being alone with her very much, although she gave no trouble; there seemed to be something very wrong with her. Sometimes she whispered to herself, too quietly for me to hear.

In the afternoon I made her rest. When she looked as if she was asleep I went to the village to see if I could get a woman who would live in the house and help a little. On my way I passed the man with the Cochin hens. He was making a beehive from pale new wood, and long curls of shavings lay about his feet. I went to the house where they sold vegetables; but they knew no one who would work for Mrs. Peebles—the woman quickly shut the door in my face, making it quite clear that no one would want to work at the house.

At the village shop, with its summer postcards, plain and coloured, hanging like curtains in the windows, it was the same, although I bought some matches to give me courage before I asked for their help.

"Oh no, Miss," the woman stood back from the counter and looked reproachfully at me through steel-rimmed spectacles that were almost square, "no, Miss, you won't find anyone wanting to work at The Burnt House." I told her the house wasn't burnt any more and we only lived in the top part; but she shook her head, and said, "I think you'd find it better to advertise in the London papers, Miss, if you are needing extra help." Then she wasn't looking at me any more, and I felt dismissed.

As I left the shop I heard a car coming towards me and thought it was probably Nicholas. I could hardly bear to look and see them together, and her burnished hair and lovely face. I looked, and he was alone, perhaps on his way to visit me. Frantically, I waved; forgetting my shyness, I ran into the road waving. He stopped and asked if I wanted a lift. "I was just going your way." I climbed into the car and exclaimed, "How awful if you had come for me and I'd been out."

Nicholas drove for a minute before saying, "I wasn't exactly coming to see you. I'm looking for a farmer I want to borrow some horses from and they told me he's somewhere down your lane—but, of course, I was hoping I'd see you." He turned towards me as he spoke and I knew he wasn't speaking the truth, and my brief happiness had gone.

We got out of the car and walked across a field together. Although Nicholas talked to me in his usual light, teasing manner, it wasn't the same between us any more, and I was glad when we reached the farmer. He was a dark man, with ferrets in his pocket—more like a poacher, I thought. While they talked I sat on a haystack, which had a great slice cut away from it. It was a comforting, sweet-smelling sort of place to be, and, as I half lay there, I had an idea. I thought, 'I'll show Nicholas I can do things others can't do.'

I heard the farmer walk away and Nicholas come round the stack towards me. My eyes were closed to concentrate better. He said my name, but I stayed quite still until I felt myself rising. I smiled to myself: I felt so light and free. I knew Nicholas was standing still beside me.

Then I heard him say in a scared and awful whisper, "Christ! Stop it, stop it, I say!"

I opened my eyes and turned towards him. Our faces were on a level, only mine was horizontal. His face looked white and dreadful, with an expression almost as if he thought me vile and infamous. I fell back on the hay and lay there quite straight and we stared at each other. Then he turned away and muttered, "You had better come, if you're coming." I answered that I wasn't coming; I'd just stay where I was for a time, and he went away without looking back. I listened to his car starting and driving off until I could hear it no more.

The last time I saw Nicholas was the following day. He was riding with his girl again on the edge of the little wood. I stood in the road watching them, and, although I was far away, I could see them quite clearly cantering in the sun and sudden shadow.

There had hardly been time for Blinkers to answer my letter, but I kept hoping he would come and help me with Mrs. Peebles. Every morning I'd walk down the lane a little way to see if he was coming, but it was always empty and I'd return to find his mother sitting still and stony-eyed, sometimes talking to herself, but never to me. She became repulsive to me, like some old brown flower, and one afternoon I couldn't bear it any more. I ran outside to the caravan and lay there listening to the sandpipers and an occasional sea-gull. I couldn't even cry because I hated myself so much. I thought I heard someone else crying, though. Somehow I resented their sorrow, as if only I were entitled to it; but then I was ashamed of my utter selfishness and opened the caravan door and listened. No one was crying now, and I thought I'd imagined it. I leant over the half-door and saw the creek had filled with water. It was high tide and the spring wind blew my hair away from my face, and I felt refreshed and clean.

I hurried across the grass to the house. Mrs. Peebles was no longer repulsive to me. I wanted to forget myself and comfort her. I could imagine the poor thing sitting so still and brown and sad. The greenhouse door was open, and so was the stained-glass one that led into the house. There was Shakespeare's head gently swinging to and fro, and light streamed down through the grated ceiling into the hall. I walked across to the clanking stairs.

Clank, clank my feet on the stairs; clank, clank on the landing. All the doors are open. One of Mrs. Peebles's black shoes is caught in the ironwork and abandoned. Through the open doors are rooms with open windows, and it is like a zoo with the animals let loose and escaped. No one is there. "Mrs. Peebles, where are you?" Where are you? Not upstairs or below, or in the garden where you never went. Where are you? For a long time I look for her, even in the green shed, but she isn't there hanging from the roof with the rope cutting into her brown neck.

I run down the lane, leaving the house with its open doors and windows, and I find the man with the Cochin hens, which shine white and enormous in the dark shed. I tell him Mrs. Peebles is missing. At first he doesn't understand; then slowly he says, "You don't mean her that roped herself up—not her that's dotty?" I tell him, "Yes," and he thinks and says, "That's bad. Do you want me to help find her?" And I said "Yes" again, and he comes with me to The Burnt House. Together we look in all the places I've looked in before, and I call, "Where are you, Mrs. Peebles?" and there is no answer. The man says, "That's bad," again, and he thinks and chews tobacco, and his spit is brown. Then I am alone while he goes to the village to get more people to join in the search. I stay behind in case she returns, perhaps wearing only one shoe.

I walk down to the creek and look towards the boat-yard. She is not there, nor coming towards me along the little waterside path. Then I go on the jetty to gain a better view; but everywhere is deserted and quiet, and the wind has become cold. Slowly I leave the jetty. Then one of my feet kicks something black. It is the other shoe, Mrs. Peebles's pointed shoe, the fellow to the one on the landing. Now she has no shoes, and she couldn't walk far without shoes. Perhaps she has gone no farther. I look into the water, but it is just dark and empty and little sharp waves. Smack, smack, quite sharp against the dinghy and the posts that support the jetty, and as I walk away I still hear it in my head. "Smack, smack. Where are you, Mrs. Peebles?"

Mrs. Peebles was dead—dead and drowned. People came from the village and found her, although they wouldn't help before. They discovered her underneath the water. I sat in the house with a policeman who asked me questions about her and about the

Gowleys. He was kind, and asked, "Do you mind if I smoke?" So I sat with the smoking policeman while they took Mrs. Peebles from the water. He comforted me and said it was better she should die by drowning than hanging, and he was quite right; but I knew in my heart I could have helped her more. They sent her to hospital although she was dead, and I went with the policeman to his little house, red-bricked and very clean. Homing pigeons that had failed to return were in a box beside the fire, waiting to be claimed.

I stayed the night at the policeman's house. Then Blinkers came to the Island, a sad and stunned Blinkers, with no word of reproach for me, only for himself and the Gowleys. There was an inquest, which I had to attend. Although they let me sit down when I gave evidence, my teeth chattered and shivering came. Outside the sparrows chirped very loud. I tried to think of them, but instead I thought of Mrs. Peebles and how I hadn't comforted her. I wondered if she was folded up in the water when they found her, or lying flat and at rest.

Chapter Eighteen

BLINKERS TOOK ME HOME by train to my father, who, he said, was expecting me. How dreadful to be expected by my father! I'd rather have been expected by anyone else. I remembered him talking to Mother when she wasn't there any more, his cruel square hands and stubborn bull-like head, and I knew he was utterly terrible. And all the time the train was bringing me nearer to him. We didn't talk much, Blinkers and I. He just looked straight in front and kept sighing, and his raincoat had a black diamond sewn on the sleeve. I felt it would be unfeeling to read the magazines he had bought me, so held them on my lap and looked out of the window. All the way I could see spring was coming. There would be no spring at home except for the blackbird singing in the dirty holly tree.

We drove from the station in a cab, a slow jolting drive. Then I was home, and, as soon as the door opened, there was the same old smell of animals. Mrs. Churchill stood waiting rather sadly, and her face looked as if it had been rubbed with ashes, as if for Ash Wednesday, only it was Friday. She welcomed me, but she seemed put out by something. Blinkers and the cab-driver followed me into the hall, she gave the cab-driver an extra sixpence to carry the great trunk up to my room, and we stood in the hall watching him struggle with the black object. Then I asked her where the parrot was. I'd missed its usual screaming welcome; perhaps it had died. Her face worked in an odd way, like knitting coming undone. "She had it sent away—couldn't stand it, she said, and I'm leaving myself tomorrow. The old bird and me, she can't stand us."

So 'she' was back—'she' could only mean Rosa. We all stood there in the gloomy hall; then Mrs. Churchill tottered away to the kitchen, and her shoulders were shaking with sobs. Blinkers put a macintosh-covered arm round me, and tried to draw me close. I stood beside him, straight and rigid, as he murmured close to my hair, "I'm sorry about this, Alice. It's most unfortunate, but I'll return in a few days—a week at the most. Mother's funeral, I must go home for that, although I can hardly call it home now. Good-bye, my dear girl." The macintosh arm held me even closer, and I knew that, when he returned, he would ask me to marry him and live in Earl's Court, away from my father and Rosa. I'd be safe in Earl's

Court with Blinkers and the old ladies with Pekineses, and we'd have lace curtains so that people couldn't see what was going on behind.

'Oh, Nicholas!' I thought, 'suppose I'd married you, and we had ridden horses in the sun and sailed in your little boat, and, when you were away at sea, I'd have sat in flower-covered chairs and thought about you!' Now I'd have to marry Blinkers and see him walking about in his braces—once I'd seen his bare arms, and they were strong and stout and hairy. I was crying when he left, and he thought it was because I would not see him for a week. Even humble men are conceited sometimes.

When he had gone, Rosa came out of the dining-room. She resembled a white negress more than ever; and her hair was an even brighter yellow than it used to be. She stood there smiling and tapping her heels on the floor.

"Didn't expect to see me here, did you?" she asked. And I said "No" as I wiped the wretched tears away from my face. She said, "Let's be friends, shall we? It really would be better, because your father is going to marry me. Yes, he is, and I shall be your new mamma." She put her tongue between her teeth and rolled her eyes and gave me a friendly push.

We had tea together, sitting on the kitchen-table— quite a friendly meal really. I dreaded her asking inquisitive questions about Mrs. Peebles's death; but the main topic of conversation was her coming marriage.

"We have had the banns called once already. Your father wanted the marriage to take place in a registry office, but I stood out for the church. A beautiful wine-coloured suit I'll be wearing, very long in the jacket. I'll tell you what, dear: you can be my little bridesmaid, to show there is no ill feeling. You'll like that, won't you?" I just nodded, and she went on, "I think your father is going to give me a feather boa; I must say he's behaving very nicely, very nicely indeed. My! is that the time? I don't want to be here when your father returns. He isn't half put out by you coming home—said he'd break every bone in your body. Oh, he was only joking—you know what men are."

Then she left the house and I waited for Father and to have every bone in my body broken. Mrs. Churchill had gone; I heard little Hank clatter out of the animals' room, and the slam of the front door; and then I sat alone in the dining-room, waiting. Quite soon there was the sound of his key in the door. When I heard him put his bag down on the hall-table and saw the door-knob turn, I ran to a corner of the room. He was there with his yellow gloves covering his square hands.

"Well, you snuffling little bitch, where are you?" he bellowed, as he entered the room like some terrible genie.

Slowly I came from my corner nearer and nearer to him, although I could hardly bear it. I looked at his yellow gloves and thought, 'He can't hit me in his gloves; it's not right that he should.' He caught me by my arm and pushed his swollen, wine-smelling face close to mine and said quite quietly, "I'm finished with you and your mother—finished, do you understand?" He struck me across the mouth, and I thought my teeth would be all crooked like Mother's. I covered my mouth with my hands and screamed through my fingers, "Don't, please don't!"

He shouted, "Shut up!" and, swaying forwards, gave me a violent push so that I fell to the floor. There he stood above me, swaying and dreadful and very drunk, and he was determined to break every bone in my body, and there was no escape. I called, "Oh God, help me!" And it was as if God heard.

One moment I was lying on the floor by Father's dreadful, shining black boots, and the next I was rising from the ground quite straight above Father, my feet pointing to the door and my head to the window. At first, I dared not look down in case I fell; then I turned my head slightly and looked out of the sides of my eyes.

There was Father kneeling on the floor, almost as if he were praying. His eyes had rolled back so far that they were all white, with no pupils showing, and he was drooling at the mouth. Then in a thin, whining voice, he called, "Alice, I won't hurt you. I was drunk and didn't know what I was doing. Come down, there's a good girl! Forgive me, Alice!"

I moved to another part of the room, and his eyes followed me. "Alice!" he pleaded. I knew I was losing my strength and I'd have to come down; so I relaxed and, closing my eyes, slowly drifted down. For a moment I lay on the floor, feeling completely exhausted. It must have been the longest time I'd been in the air like that. When I opened my eyes, I still felt slightly dazed. At first, I couldn't see Father. I slowly got to my feet, and then I saw him, completely collapsed in a chair. I knew that for the time, at least, all danger of having every bone in my body broken had passed. Father wasn't fierce any more, just a buckled-up old man.

I went upstairs to my old room on the half-landing. It was just as it had always been except for the presence of the big black trunk. I lay on my bed until I heard Rosa return; then I sat on the edge, wondering what would happen next. I heard her angry voice shouting at Father, and a few minutes later she called me downstairs. We went into the kitchen together to

prepare a meal for ourselves, nothing for Father.
"Let the silly bastard sleep it off," said Rosa.

The next morning before surgery Father sent for me.
I went to his room, shaking with fear. He was sitting
at his organ-like desk chewing one of his violet
cachous, and there was a look of reflection on his face,
not anger. I stood by the door so that there was a
chance to escape if the interview went very badly.

"Sit down, Alice," he said, almost politely, not as
he'd ever spoken to me before. I sat on the nearest
chair and waited in a sinister silence only broken by the
dogs barking in the other room. He suddenly looked
at me and spoke:

"I'm sorry I wasn't myself when you returned
yesterday, very sorry." Then he paused and picked at
the quicks of his finger-nails. "Alice," he continued,
"you behaved very strangely yesterday . . . er . . . it
was most peculiar." Peculiar! that word again. "You
seemed to leave the ground in the most extraordinary
manner and . . . er . . . actually appeared to float in the
air. I'd be very interested to see you do this again. If
you would just lie down on that piece of carpet there
and show me what you can do."

I said, "Oh no, Father, I really don't want to.
People don't like it, you know. They think it's
peculiar. Oh, please, I don't want to be peculiar!"

Father looked annoyed and I half rose up from my chair.

"No, sit down!" he commanded. "Tell me, have others witnessed this strange performance of yours?"

I answered, "Well, only one person has seen me. I only went up a little way, and he was quite horrified. I never spoke to him again, but I know he didn't like it—he was kind of disgusted with me."

"Who was this person who saw you?"

"Well," I answered, "he was only a young man on the Island. No one else was there—unless the man with a ferret saw, too."

"Oh, well, locals—what can you expect? Although it is rather a startling sight if one isn't prepared—yes, quite startling. I expect you noticed I was rather upset at the time. Nevertheless, I would like you to go to that piece of carpet and show what you can do."

Reluctantly, I left my seat and walked towards the carpet. I turned to Father.

"Are you sure you want me to be peculiar like that?" I said.

"Yes, quite sure," he snapped, "and be quick about it. I'm tired of all this shilly-shallying." He belched and mopped his brow with his handkerchief. "Something seems to have given me indigestion, although I haven't eaten a thing." Then fiercely, "Now, then, hurry up!"

So I lay on the carpet, which smelt of disinfectant, and willed myself to rise. Each time I did this thing it became easier; but I felt a sort of guilt and wished this floating had never happened to me. I went up quite quickly, and stayed still, with my face almost touching the ceiling. I'd always heard heat rises, and I found it quite true; although it was quite a cool day, I found it unbelievably stuffy up there and hoped Father wouldn't expect me to stay long. I looked down on him, sitting at his desk, watching me intently.

He asked, "Can you move—I mean move to another part of the room?"

I floated as far away from the window as I could so that people in the street wouldn't see me; then I asked if I could come down. It was very exhausting, and the extra effort of speaking made it worse. I couldn't wait for his reply. I came down so suddenly it rather hurt my back and I lay some time on the floor with my eyes shut. When I opened them, Father was standing by me, and he helped me up into a chair.

Chapter Nineteen

FATHER HELPING ME into a chair was typical of the days that followed. There were other things quite unlike anything that had happened to me at home before. For instance, Rosa brought me breakfast in bed every morning. At first she was annoyed about this and stood glowering at me from the end of the bed, iron curlers standing savagely on her head. For some reason, her marriage to Father was put off for a few weeks, which distressed her considerably, and she thought I was to blame. Then suddenly she was all smiles and sweetness. She cooked me delicious meals, kept forcing glasses of milk on to me because, she said, I needed feeding up; manicured my nails, and brushed my pale hair until it became a shining helmet. Whenever I left the house, she came with me, as if she couldn't bear me out of her sight.

I wanted to visit Lucy, but I knew her mother wouldn't welcome Rosa, so we just walked past her house. In the front garden was a frightful little buckled-up pram, vibrating with the screams of a new-born baby. Rosa said it was Lucy's baby. I said no one had told me she was married, and Rosa gave a shriek of laughter. "Married, my foot!" she exclaimed. "Who would marry such a half-witted deaf and dumb creature? No, that's a bastard brat, and I'm telling you now: your father won't have you seeing that Lucy any more."

So the gentle Lucy had had a bastard like any common girl. I could hardly believe it, but there was no one to ask now Mrs. Churchill had gone. Then I thought, 'Well, if it's true, at least Lucy has her baby, and I'd have been glad to have had Nicholas's baby, even if we hadn't been married.' Then I felt afraid of myself for having such wicked thoughts.

I ate my meals with Father and Rosa now. "Do you fancy a little of the white meat, dear?" Rosa would say. And Father would pour me out a glass of red wine and say, "There is nothing like wine to build you up." After dinner it would be, "You go upstairs and have a nice little rest. I'll clear away and wash up, and later we might take a stroll on the common." And Father would add, "Yes, fresh air's good for the girl. But, mind you, she's not to leave the house if there is a sign of rain; we can't have her getting wet."

Two friends of Father's kept coming to the house now—Frink and Sully they were called. Frink was a middle-aged German with straight grey hair sticking up like a dirty toothbrush; I think he was a watch-repairer. Sully was fat, with big creases in his face and wisps of sandy hair and a greasy voice. His moist and flabby hands were always touching Rosa when Father wasn't there, and he would put his squashy face close to hers and she would scream, "Oh, Mr. Sully, you mustn't do that!" then clap her hand over her mouth in case Father heard. He owned a local paper, and Rosa said he was a very important gentleman and entitled to take a few liberties. Fortunately, he didn't take any with me. He was respectful; but his little blue eyes used to follow me round and on his face there was a strange, sort of calculating, expression.

Then I realised Sully and Frink were coming to the house because of my floating (only they always called it by its proper name—levitation). One evening Father ordered me into his room and told me they would be very interested to see what I could do. I didn't want them to see me do this thing, looking at me with their big coarse faces and fat, buried eyes; but Father insisted that I should. He drew the curtains, and there I was, enclosed with these men and tobacco smoke and gaslight. I thought, 'The only thing I can do is get it over quickly.' I lay down, but because I felt this way and was not relaxed, it wouldn't happen at first. Father became angry, and Sully and Frink exchanged glances. Suddenly, Father rushed towards me with his eyes bulging in a terrifying way and snarling like a fighting dog. I went up quickly enough then. I stayed there with my face close to the ceiling, feeling worried about my skirt hanging down and my drawers most likely showing. The men below seemed very upset. Sully was sobbing and Frink muttering away to himself in German. Father was dumbfounded—not by me, but the way these men were behaving. When I came down, they still hadn't recovered. So I left them with Father, who was trying to revive them with whisky and water.

Although my levitation had had such a strange effect on these men, they couldn't see enough of it. They kept pestering Father for another demonstration, then another, although I heard Father say he didn't want me to be worn out already. It was true I was becoming worn out. Sometimes, after I'd done this thing for them, I'd fall asleep on the floor and stay like that for an hour; and often I'd find Rosa and my father had carried me upstairs to my room and I'd be lying on my bed when I awoke. In spite of all the extra food I was made to eat I was tired all the time.

One evening, when it was almost dark, they made me rise up in the garden. I was afraid, afraid of the house and high walls all round, and the clinkers that lay below. Even the cry of the newsboys and the street sounds were terrible up there in the near darkness. When I came down, I was so exhausted, they gave me red wine to drink. I could feel it running down my chin when I woke up. I remembered coming down in the garden and my back rather hurting, and then I was in the kitchen with warm wine running down my chin. I thought I'd injured myself and it must be blood.

I said, "I knew no good could ever come of this," but they ignored me. Frink was talking in his guttural way about the levitating Mr. Home. Sully dismissed him as a religious crank, and said the beauty of my case was, I wasn't religious. He seemed to think I was going to make them rich. I could not think how this could come about, but I knew it must be something bad they were planning.

Blinkers came to the house. I wasn't allowed to see him, although I heard his voice in the hall. I was in the kitchen at the time, and Rosa made me go into the pantry and bolted the door on me. I kicked and shouted, not because I particularly wanted to see Blinkers, but because it was like prison in there— damp and airless and smelling of sour bread and cockroaches. There were angry men's voices in the hall. Father had wanted Blinkers to take me away, but now he wouldn't let him see me. It must be because I was valuable to him in some way to do with this levitation and Sully and Frink. I pondered on these things while

I half-heartedly kicked the door, and I became afraid.

When Blinkers had gone, Rosa let me out. She said it was a bloody shame: she wouldn't have done it, only Father had ordered her to lock me up if that 'Peebles fellow' turned up—she couldn't tell me why. I told her Blinkers didn't mean a thing to me except that he had always been kind. Then, in my loneliness, I told her how I'd loved Nicholas. I tried to describe the careless beauty that surrounded him with a golden haze, and, as I spoke of Nicholas, I forgot it was Rosa I was speaking to—until she interrupted me with screams of laughter and said I'd be the death of her. I deeply regretted I'd ever mentioned Nicholas to her. It was strange she said I'd be the 'death of her', because in a way I was.

After Blinkers's visit I became a sort of prisoner, with Rosa as my rather unwilling jailer; I even slept in her room. Sully and Frink were in and out of the house all the time, and I became more and more afraid because I knew it was because of me that they came. Then one day Rosa showed me a newspaper—the one that Sully owned. In deep black type there was an announcement to say that Miss Alice was going to give an amazing demonstration on Clapham Common on Sunday afternoon. It gave the date and the exact place on the Common where the demonstration was going to take place; but it omitted to say what Miss Alice was going to demonstrate. Then Father called me into his dreadful room. He told me that I was Miss Alice. I was to rise up before all the people on the Common, and the result would be that I'd be showered with offers to appear in circuses and music-halls all over England—and the world, too, perhaps.

"Rise up before people on the Common and in music-halls and circuses! Please God, don't let that happen to me. Father, don't make me do this thing. I don't want to be peculiar and different. I want to be an ordinary person. I'll marry Henry Peebles and go away and you needn't see me any more—but don't make me do this terrible thing."

I cried to God and to my father, but it was printed there in Sully's paper and there was no escape.

The days that followed this announcement were like a nightmare, unreal and terrible. All the unexpected kindness and care which had come my way so recently were like a fattening up before I was slaughtered. I fretted and couldn't eat, so Rosa held my nose while Father forced minced chicken and beef down my throat. Then my nose became discoloured and swollen as a result of this rough treatment, and Sully said I wouldn't do them much credit with a nose like that, so the forcible feeding ceased and I lived on raw eggs beaten up in milk. Sully and Frink wanted me to have what they called a 'preliminary canter' on the Common before Sunday, but, to my relief, Father refused. I think he thought I'd float right away—which is what I would have done if I had had the strength.

At night I lay in Mother's old room. It was now all pink, and belonged to Rosa. I lay stretched out beside Rosa, who was rather bony, and her hair, which was like dry wool, was on the pillow beside me. My eyes stayed wide open, and I was so rigid that my jaw ached and felt as if it were locked. Sometimes I must have slept, but the nights seemed interminable. I kept imagining how it would be on the Common. I'd see a white and glaring sky and feel the aching tiredness of trying to remain above a gaping crowd, above all their round faces and open, toothless mouths, and noses that pointed up towards me. Then I'd think I heard them shrieking with laughter. Sometimes I'd be on the ground struggling to rise, but pulled back as if by great bands of elastic; my father and Sully would be urging me on, and Frink looking at me intently through a magnifying glass. If I did manage to doze off for a few minutes, I'd dream I was falling and wake with a start, my heart pounding. I knew that, whatever happened on the Common, life would be dreadful for me afterwards. If I failed to levitate myself, I'd be publicly disgraced and probably murdered by my father; but if I managed to do this thing, I'd be branded as peculiar and separated from ordinary people for ever. I'd be a kind of peep-show, a poor freak travelling the country, and people would press close and gape at me.

I began to long for Blinkers and Mrs. Churchill, Blinkers in particular because I knew he had more power to help me. I remembered the selfless kindness he had always shown me and the feeling of safeness about him. I thought that, if only he would come to the house now, I'd gladly go away with him for life. I used to call him to myself 'that Blinkard', but now he seemed to me a sort of hero—even if rather a round and sturdy one. I'd try not to mind the stodginess of him or the thick hairy arms if only he would save me.

In the night, when Rosa was asleep, I wrote to him on a sheet of paper that had lined the drawers that held my clothes.

"Henry, save me!" I wrote. "They are going to make me float on the Common and in music-halls all over the world. I want to be ordinary. Please save me, Blinkers."

I wrote this with a pencil intended for Rosa's brows, and I made an envelope and closed it with a pin. During the morning I gave this home-made letter to little Hank to post. He was worried about the absence of a stamp and I had difficulty in making him promise to post it, but eventually he clumped off with a couple of dogs, eating a hunk of bread and treacle I'd bribed him with. When he returned, I ran into the hall and examined his pockets to make sure the letter was really gone.

Rosa came into the hall, shouting, "What are you doing with that snivelling kid?"

I answered that he was a good boy really, and couldn't he have a cup of tea with us in the kitchen; and so we sat there together in the kitchen, Hank never saying a word. I felt almost happy because I knew, if Blinkers received that letter, I would be saved.

Sunday morning came. I awoke from a late dream that I was being submerged in a pit of cobwebs made of dank mud. Even when I saw Rosa standing there in her long night-gown with the morning light shining on her high cheek-bones, I thought, as I struggled from my dream, 'There is still time for Blinkers to save me. All I must do is keep calm until he comes.'

They wanted me to stay in bed all the morning. I was locked in the bedroom and treated rather like a reluctant bride. I didn't panic, but just lay there waiting for Blinkers.

He did not come.

Chapter Twenty

THEY GAVE ME SHERRY beaten up with eggs and milk.
They dressed me in a long white dress I'd never seen
before, and white silk stockings that were soft against
my legs. Rosa put rouge upon my cheeks, they were
so pale. All rouged and dressed in white, I was taken
downstairs by Rosa. She was wearing a large hat filled
with roses, and a watch upon a chain given her by
Father. They said I was to have one, too, if I did all
they told me on the Common. I did not want a watch,
or care about time. I stood there in the hall with Sully
and Frink and Rosa until the carriage drove up to the
house. Yelping followed Father as he opened the door
of the animals' room and came to join us. They half
carried me into the closed carriage. Now I knew there
was no escape for me and I'd got to go through with
this thing.

We drove up Lavender Hill, past closed shops and
people wearing Sunday clothes. We bowled along
in silence—except for Sully, who pushed his flabby

face close to mine and said, "Keep calm, Missy; but remember, we are depending on you."

I turned away from him and looked out of the windows at the great grey houses of Cedars Road. Father impatiently pulled the blinds down. I could tell he was nervous, because his face was drenched in sweat; and Sully wasn't feeling happy either: his great baby face was all twitching. Only Frink sat still and remote. Rosa was uneasily fidgeting with her feather boa and looking from one to the other of the men, bewildered by their silence. She had never seen me float and I don't think she believed I really did this thing; it was just some trick of my father's that was going to make us all rich. Now the tense atmosphere of that hearse-like carriage made her uneasy.

We left the carriage on the north side of the Common, near the old church with the blue-faced clock. Slowly we walked over the grass, where every now and then there was a dandelion in flower. Rosa held my arm and, as if in a dream, I walked beside her, the three bowler-hatted men following and arguing about exactly where this fearful thing was to take place.

It must have been raining earlier in the day because the grass was very wet. Now the sky was a lit-up silver, and there was a soft west wind. We must have been a strange group because people kept turning to glance at us and some said we were a wedding-party and I was the bride, dressed in white as I was, and there were flowers in my hair. Grown men and boys were flying kites, and I feared that perhaps later on I would become entangled in their strings. We came to the green-domed bandstand, and heard the orators' shouting voices blowing towards us on the wind.

"Too many trees here," Father said to Frink.

We walked past the park-keepers' bothy and the old men playing chess in the shelter; the same old men seemed to have been playing the same game of chess there all the years I could remember, in winter and summer. We left these things behind and came into the open again. I could see the two great grey mansions against the silver sky. When I was a child, I thought they were something holy from the Bible—'In my Father's house there are many mansions.' Now, although I knew they were not holy, the huge and familiar greyness of them comforted me.

Rosa suddenly pinched my arm. I turned to her and saw it was her sad clown's face she was wearing, all pinched and with the powder standing out on it.

" 'Ere," she said, and her voice was a thin, Cockney whine that I'd never heard her use before. " 'Ere, all this is giving me the pip. Let's go 'ome. I don't like it." She loosened her hold on my arm and turned to Father. "Euan Rowlands," she wailed, "take us 'ome; this is 'orrible!"

185

Father ignored her and turned to Sully and Frink. "This will do," he said, in a low voice, and we all stood still. "Yes, this will do," they agreed. "It's away from the trees and near enough to the speakers. Yes, this will do." And Frink, in his guttural voice, muttered, "Not too many people—we don't want a stampede."

They made me lie down on the grass, although it was all wet and dirty.

"My dress," I whispered, "my long white dress, it won't be white any more."

"Never mind about that," Father snarled at me. "Just lie there and relax."

So I lay there in my despair and humiliation. People who saw me thought I'd fainted and gathered round; I was so conspicuous in my white dress. More people, from the outskirts of the crowd by the orators, hurried over the grass towards me. It was like when drops of water seem to magnetise each other and draw together. Rosa was crying, her back turned to me and her thin shoulders under the feather boa vibrating. Sully and Frink had drawn away, to be able to escape quickly if things went wrong. Only Father was close to me, and his face was terrible. He almost screamed at me, "Go on, do it now! For Christ's sake, don't let us down! Hurry!"

Someone was bending down to help me and I could

have saved myself, but Father's terrible face was before me, and I made a frantic effort simply to escape the horror of my father. I went up quite straight, about ten feet into the air, and then a little higher. I stayed quite still up there, and there was a dreadful silence. All those people—it was as if they were dead, so still they were, and I could hear a whizzing bee. The silence only lasted an instant, then a great roar came, and screams and cries—animal noises. I looked below and there they were, not animals but hundreds of milling people. Some were shouting and pointing upwards at me, and others were on their knees, praying. A few were running away, not straight but in circles.

Then I caught sight of two rather stout figures hurrying towards the crowd. Their anguished faces were turned up towards me and I recognised Mrs. Churchill and Blinkers, Blinkers no longer wearing a black diamond now, but dressed in complete blackness, like a parson. My two stout friends—too late to save me! On the outskirts of the crowd I thought I saw Lucy's gentle face, and a lolling baby in her arms.

Waves of tiredness passed through me, and I descended a few feet. Grabbing hands stretched towards me, but I willed myself to rise higher because I was so afraid of falling on the people. I did manage for a little to float horizontally away from the crowd; but, when I next looked down, they were all below me again. I was so exhausted I knew I could not stay above them much longer. Soon I'd be down amongst them. I felt I was gradually losing consciousness and tried to signal with one hand that I was coming down.

I could hear Father's voice shouting, "Make way!" and, as I sailed down, although my eyes were closed, I could feel the crowd had opened and there was a clearing below me.

I came down amongst the people. Although we were out of doors the air was stuffy and sickening. When I opened my eyes, all I could see was feet and cloth-encased legs. Then the shouting started again, and the feet and legs commenced to sway and jostle, and there were angry exclamations and cries of pain. The space around me began to close. The people from behind pushed and shoved and the feet came nearer. Suddenly I saw a man with a ginger moustache staring at me with a terrified expression on his face. I tried to smile at him because I felt he needed pity, poor man— and I'd seen him before. But in a moment he was pushed to the ground, the advancing crowd falling over his body. I tried to leave the ground, and caught at Rosa's skirt. Poor thing! she was standing there screaming, with her hands over her face. They must have seen the white of my dress because a cry of "There she is!" from many voices, sounding like one great voice, poured into my ears. As they pressed forward, Rosa lost her balance and, still screaming, fell across me. I thought I could distinguish Father's voice as he tried to keep them back, but still they pressed forward, the ones in front unable to help themselves. I managed to turn my face to one side, but I was pinned down by Rosa's body and couldn't free my hands to protect my face.

The terrible feet came, and no air at all could reach me. I could still hear Rosa screaming as they trampled and fell on me, and there was the indescribable pain. Then I could feel nothing. I simply thought, 'This is it; this is how one dies.' Rosa had ceased to scream, and for the first time in my life I was not afraid.

The following newspaper report—one among many that appeared at the time—refers to the incident described at the end of this book:

"*The inquest was held today on the three people recently trampled to death by a crowd on Clapham Common. The victims were Alice Rowlands and Rosa Fisher, both of Battersea, and a man so far unidentified.*

"*From the evidence, it appears that Alice Rowlands pretended to be able to levitate herself and the accident occurred when a crowd watching a performance of the trick got out of control. The girl appeared on the Common dressed as a bride, and several witnesses insisted that she had raised herself to a considerable height above the ground.*

"The police stated that they had been unable to obtain any information from the girl's father, who had been seriously ill since witnessing the occurrence."

BARBARA COMYNS

was born at Bidford-on-Avon, Warwickshire, in 1909.
She was mainly educated by governesses until she went
to art schools in Stratford-on-Avon and London. She
has worked in an advertising agency, a typewriting
bureau, dealt in old cars and antique furniture, bred
poodles, converted and let flats and has exhibited
pictures at The London Group. She was married first in
1931, to an artist, and for the second time in 1945 to her
present husband with whom she lived in Spain for
eighteen years.

She started writing fiction at the age of ten and her
first novel, *Sisters by a River*, was published in 1947.
Since then she has published seven novels: *Our Spoons
came from Woolworths* (1950), *Who Was Changed and Who
Was Dead* (1955), *The Vet's Daughter* (1959), *Out of the
Red into the Blue* (1960), *The Skin Chairs* (1962), *Birds in
Tiny Cages* (1964), and *A Touch of Mistletoe* (1967).
The Vet's Daughter is her best known novel, and has
been both serialised and dramatised by BBC Radio.
Sandy Wilson turned it into a musical called *The
Clapham Wonder* which was performed at the Marlowe
Theatre, Canterbury in 1978. Barbara Comyns has one
son, one daughter and five grandchildren. She lives in
Richmond, Surrey, with her husband.